MIDNIGHT ARCADE

ARCADE

Crypt Quest/Space Battles

by Gabe Soria
art by Kendall Hale

Penguin Workshop
An Imprint of Penguin Random House

DIRECTIONS

One thing you'll learn quickly here is that it's not always easy to follow the instructions. You never know when the game . . . I mean, the book . . . is going to send you to your doom. But if you want a truly exhilarating experience, you'll need to do exactly what the book tells you . . . except, of course, when you get to make a choice. In these cases, you should trust your gut.

When you see a game controller like the one below, you'll be presented with multiple options to move around or take an action. Once you make a choice, turn to the corresponding page and find the matching symbol.

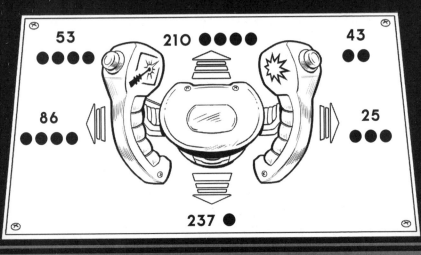

There can be as many as four sections on a page, so make sure you ONLY read the one marked with your symbol for that page.

At times, you'll be sent to a page and symbol without a choice. Do as you're instructed to keep the story flowing correctly.

Sometimes you'll make a wrong choice, and the game will end. At that time, you'll have a choice to either restart that level or exit the Midnight Arcade.

There are countless ways to read this book . . . I mean, play these games . . . I mean, read this book . . . I mean . . . Well, you get the picture. Have fun, and good luck!

Welcome to the
MIDNIGHT ARCADE ☽

As you stand in front of the boarded-up doors that loom before you, you can't help but wonder: *Am I nuts?* You turn around and see your friends, who are standing behind a chain-link fence one hundred yards away, looking at you expectantly, with wonder and a little bit of awe, because you're actually DOING IT—you're about to enter the abandoned Fair Oaks Mall.

FAIR
OAKS
MALL

GAME
OVER

Located at the edge of town, the mall has been empty for pretty much an ETERNITY (since 1990 at least), and ever since it closed and started to fall apart, it's become legendary, a haunted house made up of dusty old clothes stores and forgotten fast-food franchises. The kids at your school have been daring one another to enter for years, but as far as you know, nobody's ever been brave enough to actually go IN.

Until tonight. Until you.

Earlier in the evening, as the rest of the town slept, you and your friends snuck out of your houses and rode your bikes out to the mall. But when the time came to hop the rusty fence that surrounds the derelict shopping center, everybody else chickened out. Except you. You scaled the ten-foot-tall chain-link fence and crossed the cracked pavement of the weed-strewn parking lot. And now it's the moment of truth.

"Come on!" you hear one of your friends yell.

"We don't have all night!" says another one.

Ignoring them, you open the backpack you're carrying, pulling out a hammer, which you use to pry the nails out of the boards in front of you. Pausing for a moment, you notice that someone has sloppily scrawled the words GAME OVER in bloodred spray paint on the wood. The boards fall to the ground with a clatter, and you stand before the entrance to the shopping center, gazing into the darkness beyond the cracked glass doors that lead inside. You glance over your shoulder. Your friends are still standing on the other side of the fence. Nobody's making funny comments now. They're staring at you in disbelief. *Are you REALLY going to go in there?* their worried expressions ask. In answer, you give them a thumbs-up and take a flashlight out of the backpack. You point it at your friends and click it on and off and on again to signal them. With a farewell wave, you cross the threshold of the entrance and plunge into the darkness.

Inside the mall, it's almost totally silent; you can hear the slow *drip-drip-drip* of water leaking somewhere, but otherwise, it's deathly quiet. As you walk farther inside, you shine your flashlight on a greeting-card store, a shop that used to sell candles, a corny clothing boutique—all of them grimy and sad. To hear your parents talk about it, back in the '80s, the mall used to be the coolest spot in the WORLD to hang out. Now it's just an old ruin. *What a waste of time,* you think as you turn to leave. *Time to get outta here.*

And that's when you hear it, something that almost makes you jump out of your skin—it's quiet at first, and distant, but it's there: the unmistakable electronic *bleeping* and *blooping* sounds of . . . video games. And not just any video games; it sounds like old-school, vintage games, the kind you've played on arcade emulators on your computer. It's far-off, but it's somewhere in the mall. Shining your flashlight ahead, you notice a mall directory nearby and quickly find the name of the only place that could be the source of the sound: the Midnight Arcade, which is located all the way in the very back of the mall. But . . . how could there be sounds coming from an arcade that's been closed since before you were born?

Excited by the mystery, and all thoughts of leaving the mall forgotten, you plunge deeper into the darkness, toward the strange sounds, which get gradually louder the farther you go.

Soon, you come to a rusty old escalator and bound up its steps two at a time. The sound of electric mayhem gets louder, and you can make out lights flashing ahead. Feeling a little bit scared now, you slowly walk forward until you see it: a lit neon sign that reads MIDNIGHT ARCADE above the wide-open doors of a video game emporium. Inside, you can see the source of the sounds you've been hearing: All the games are turned on . . . even though the power is out everywhere else in the mall. Weird doesn't even begin to cover it. Your brain is telling you that this is unnatural and that you should probably leave, but your curiosity wins out over logic, and you decide to keep going. Moments later, you've entered the arcade.

Once inside, crazy sounds and flashing lights bombard your senses. This is nothing like playing games at home. Here, every game is ready to be played, and each seems to be trying to lure you in. You could almost swear that out of the corner of your eye you see the ghosts of people standing around the machines and playing them, but when you turn, there's nobody there. *Pretty creepy,* you think.

As you wander through the arcade, going deeper into its mazelike depths, you're overwhelmed by the sheer amount of games inside its walls, games that you feel like you should recognize; but you've got to admit that while they seem familiar, you've never actually heard of *any* of them. *Mass Scott? Wrestlevania? Mow-Town?* You've done a lot of vintage-game playing in your time, but none of the names on the cabinets ring a bell. *Have I discovered a cache of obscure games?* you wonder. *Some collector's secret stash?* You take out your phone to snap some pictures as evidence to show your friends, but the battery's dead, which is weird—you distinctly remember it being at 100 percent when you left the house earlier. Another mystery, but that can wait. It's time to go.

You begin to trace your steps back toward the front door, but the labyrinth of games is confusing: Was the entrance to the left, past the change machine? Or was it to the right, past the alley of pinball machines? Turning a corner, you suddenly realize something terrifying: You are not alone. Standing there in front of you, blocking the doors, is a young man . . . kind of. Dressed in sneakers, jeans, and a baseball T-shirt with the Midnight Arcade logo on it, and wearing a jingling money-changing belt around his waist, this guy looks, well, like he's not quite real. He's not a ghost or a zombie or anything like that, but he doesn't seem entirely human, either.

"Welcome to the Midnight Arcade," he says, suddenly standing next to you. "It's been a long time since we've had a customer. Why don't you try one of our games? Got a quarter?"

You feel strangely compelled to reach into your pocket and fish around for a coin, which you produce and then hand to the mysterious attendant.
Smiling, he drops it into one of his pockets and presses down on one of the levers of the contraption attached to his belt. He hands something to you, and you see that it's shiny—a shiny TOKEN that looks like this:

You smile as you clutch it tightly in your fist. *Now I'll have evidence to show everybody I was in here*, you think.

"That token's not for collecting; it's for playing," the attendant says, almost as if he's read your mind. He grins and then points over your shoulder. Turning, you see two video game cabinets before you, games that you could swear weren't there a second ago. A creepy mist moves slowly around them.

"Go ahead—you've got a token in your hand. It'd be a shame to waste a token."

Every instinct in your body is telling you to leave the Midnight Arcade as fast as your legs can carry you and get away from this weirdo, but something else is making you stay. After all, the games look so cool, and their attract modes are SO enticing. What harm could one game do?

Token held between your thumb and forefinger, you contemplate each of the games in front of you. Which one will you play?

If you want to play *Space Battles*, head to 129 ●
If you want to play *Crypt Quest*, head to 167 ●

●

As you pull to the left, the other pilot seems to sense what you're doing and goes in the exact opposite direction, zipping out of view. You pound your instrument panel in frustration. Lost 'em!

Head back to 23 ●

●●

You raise your sword to parry the missile of magic, and much to your surprise, it actually WORKS! Whatever enchantment your weapon holds must be proof against the Death-King's sorcery, for it deflects the beam toward the ceiling, causing rubble to rain down to the throne room floor. But the force of the impact sends your sword flying out of your hands!

Head to 153 ●

●●●

Terrified, you try to exit the Castle-Crypt, but remember too late that the bridge you ran here on no longer exists. Instead of terra firma, you find yourself trying to flee over empty air. Remember: This is a video game, not a cartoon, and you can't just run back. It's science!

Head to 242 ●●●

●●●●

KZZORCH! If nothing else, the lasers sure work! The Galactic Authority troops scatter and fly through the air, blown hither and yon by your blasts. That's bought you a few moments, but what now? Choose another action.

Head back to 56 ●●

●

You attempt to move somewhere, anywhere, to avoid the next blast from the hover tank's cannon, but no matter which direction you go, the barrel of its weapon tracks you . . . and then fires! And as it turns out, your Walker can't survive another blast. This one cripples it, causing a complete systems shutdown. The legs on the mech seize up, and the vehicle topples over, with you inside. You black out for a moment, then come to, and when you do, you see Galactic Authority troops surrounding your cockpit, weapons aimed straight at you through the cracked glass. It looks like they're waiting for the command to fire. And then one of them speaks up.

"All right . . . fire!"

And they do. Ouch.

YOU ARE DEAD. CONTINUE: Y/N?
Y: Head to 56 ●● **N: Head to 242** ●●●

C.O.B. continues his relentless run toward Slaystation Omega's control center, all the while being hounded by the Galactic Authority's Spider-Bots. Ahead, you can see another branch in the path: On the left, you can see what seems to be some sort of light, as if there is a fire raging that way. To the right, a set of stairs. Which direction do you choose?

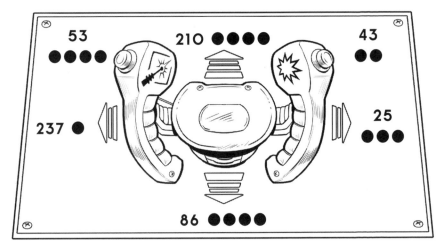

●●●

You pull your craft into a bank to the left, hoping to come around to the Black Angel's six, but the enemy ace anticipates your gambit and stays right on your tail, closing the distance between the two of you, and then . . .

BRAAP BRAAP BRAAP!

Blaster fire tears into your engines, and as your ship breaks apart, you hear the Black Angel's malicious cackle over your comms link. The last thing you ever hear and it's evil laughter. That's just great.

YOU ARE DEAD. CONTINUE: Y/N?
Y: Head to 43 ●●● N: Head to 242 ●●●

●●●●

You circle to the left around the prone body of the Death-King, waiting for some sort of treachery. In a moment, your caution proves to be wise, for the injured necromancer suddenly turns and musters up enough energy to fire another bolt of necro-magic toward you. You raise your sword again, deflecting the blow off to the side. You have another chance—what now?

Head back to 20 ●●

●

You pull up slightly, catching the Black Angel as it attempts the exact same maneuver. Your targeting guide shifts to green—it's a miracle, but you've got the Black Angel in your sights! But your celebration time is cut short as the Black Angel's ship shimmers for a moment,

then impossibly splits into an exact replica of itself!
What's going on here?!

Head to 41 ●●●

●●

Your Walker charges toward the hover tank, and as
it does, the hover tank fires its cannon, its beam just
missing the head of your Walker. Advancing as the
tank recharges, you bring the tree trunk up . . . and
then down, smashing it against the shell of the tank.
And surprisingly, THIS works! Brute force! Seeing
an opportunity, you bring the melee weapon down
again and again and again until the tank is completely
smashed. That, you think, was satisfying.

Head to 211 ●●●

●●●

After your sword pierces the chest of the Death-King, the
creature howls in dismay.

"Noooooooooo!" it cries as it backs away. "I am the
Death-King. I cannot be defeated!"

But the Death-King appears to be mistaken about
that, as your blow seems to have mortally wounded it.
Light streams from the wound in its chest, and its robes

are licked with magical flames, which spread rapidly and fiercely, The mystic fire swirls around the fiend as it protests, consuming it utterly, forming a column of energy that shoots up through the ceiling of the throne room and then vanishes, leaving only a smoldering pile of greasy, sorcerous soot on the floor.

You walk out of the throne room, being careful to avoid the many bottomless holes in its floor, and then you start to retrace your steps out of the mazelike corridors of the Castle-Crypt, slowly, tiredly. Passing through the entrance hall, you note that the possessed organ has changed its tune and is now playing a slow but rousing victory march. And with that, you know for certain that you've done it.

You've beaten *Crypt Quest*.

Leaving the Castle-Crypt, you stand and look at the scene before you. The bridge has been rebuilt by unseen hands, and the gates to the cemetery beyond are open. And just like that, you know that you have the power to leave the game if you so wish. So: What do you want to do?

If you want to play *Space Battles* now, head to 129 ●

If you want to finish your session at the Midnight Arcade, head to 242 ●●●

Your thumb presses the trigger button, unleashing a volley of laser fire in front of you, but nothing happens—you're still too far away to effectively hit any targets.

"Easy there, Cadet," says Sgt. Brixto over your comm link. "You'll get the chance to light up some Galactic Authority goons soon enough. Stay on course and stick to the mission!"

Head back to 129 ●

●

You shoot your lasers, which pass harmlessly between the two Black Angels. You'll have to do better than that, kid. Choose another tactic!

Head back to 41 ●●●

●●

"Space fighter mode unavailable," says the voice of your ship's computer. It looks like you're stuck as a cool-as-heck Walker mech for now. Enjoy, and choose again!

Head back to 166 ●●●●

●●●

Knowing you'd better try this while your Walker's arms are still free, you fire your lasers at the encroaching vines, and the blasts sever the vegetation wherever it gets hit. The separated bits flop around and quickly wither, and the vines loosen their grip and retreat.

Head to 12 ●●

●●●●

BZZT! Your special weapon fails you once again. You think that it might be time to stop using it? Maybe? No matter, because the time you wasted pressing that button was time you could have used to try to escape from the chaos all around you. Instead, you're now surrounded by impassable bottomless pits, and as the ground continues to shake, your Walker can't keep its footing, and you slip down into a crack in the jungle floor and fall down . . . down . . . down . . . down . . .

YOU ARE DEAD. CONTINUE: Y/N?
Y: Head to 56 ●● N: Head to 242 ●●●

●

Seriously? You've got the Black Angel in your crosshairs and you blow it breaking off in another direction? Have you ever heard the phrase "Snatching defeat from the jaws of victory"? Well, you have now! You probably deserve what happens next, which is piloting your ship directly into a hail of enemy fire. Alas!

YOU ARE DEAD. CONTINUE: Y/N?
Y: Head to 43 ●●● N: Head to 242 ●●●

● ●

The Walker clumsily moves to the side as the Galactic Authority hover tank trains its cannon on you, shooting an energy blast that narrowly misses you. Whether it was by accident or design, you've avoided getting a faceful of laser. Choose another action!

Head back to 166 ● ● ● ●

● ● ●

You try to rake the Black Angel with a volley of laser fire, but your opponent is just outside of your target area, and your attack passes by harmlessly. But you're still in pursuit, so try another tactic.

Head back to 235 ● ● ● ●

● ● ● ●

You break for the corridor on the left, and the Death-King standing there retreats—you picked the correct one to chase! Sword in hand, you follow.

Continue to 216 ● ● ●

●

You urge the Walker forward, and it and the Gorillosaur collide in a tangle of limbs. It's not stronger than you, but you're not stronger than it. You've reached a wrestling stalemate!

Head to 218 ● ● ● ●

● ●

Having escaped the grip of the jungle vines of death, you continue on, making progress toward the destination on the map that Sgt. Brixto sent you. You're getting closer and closer and closer, and so far, nothing else has tried to kill you . . . yet.

But once again you hear that wild howl off in the distance. *There's definitely something out there*, you think, *and it's DEFINITELY following me.* You look at your map and note with surprise that you're just about two-thirds of the way to the base. Excellent! At this rate, you'll be there in no time and maybe never get a chance to meet whatever's making that awful, awful sound.

But then, the ground beneath your Walker's feet begins to shake, almost imperceptibly at first, then with increasing—and alarming—strength. It's an earthquake! But you can handle that, right? Well, normally you could, but this is no normal earthquake, as evidenced by the cracks that begin to tear through the ground, rending the earth about you. Trees fall into newly formed chasms ahead of you, behind you, and to your right. You have to take evasive action NOW.

You must find an escape route away from the bottomless pits opening all around you. What do you do?

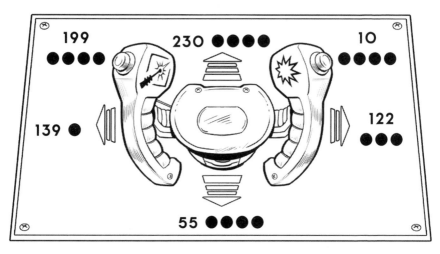

BRAAP BRAAP BRAAP BRAAP! Once again you attempt to break through the hover tank's armor with your guns, but once again you are thwarted. Energy weapons have no effect. But this does seem to have bought you some time, so pick another move!

Head back to 234 ●●●

●●●●

You attempt to use your special weapon, and . . . it
doesn't work. But what DOES work are the Gorillosaur's
legs, which it uses to leap toward you, and its arms,
which it grabs you with! You're tussling!

Head to 218 ●●●●

●

C.O.B. is ALREADY heading that way. Choose a different
action.

Head back to 153 ●●

●●

You decide to try your special weapon button, and this
time you're shocked and amazed when the targeting
reticle trained on the ship in front of you illuminates
brightly. A missile shoots from your fighter, moving back
and forth crazily as the Galactic Authority fighter tries
to evade it. But it's no use, and you can feel the impact
as the missile blows your opponent sky-high. Or is that
space-high? Either way, you got the job done.

"Excellent shot, Cadet!" you hear Sgt. Brixto say. "I
was sure you were a goner, but even ol' Sgt. Brixto gets
it wrong every once in a while. But hey—are you gonna

just sit there and pat yourself on the back, or are you gonna join the rest of us fighting this Space Battle?"

Head to 100 ●●●

●●●

The engines on the ship come to life, and your ship shudders as it begins to move forward rapidly . . . directly toward the hover tank! Before you can adjust course, you COLLIDE with the machine, causing both vehicles to combust and blow sky-high. That's one way to beat an enemy, but not a way to beat a game . . .

YOU ARE DEAD. CONTINUE: Y/N?
Y: Head to 56 ●● **N: Head to 242** ●●●

●●●●

You have the Death-King at your mercy and you decide to jump? TO JUMP?! We can't even with all of this jumping. Needless to say, your obsession with jumping has reached its natural end, and your foolishness has proved to be your undoing, as you jump yourself right into a hole in the floor of the throne room, a hole that has no bottom. *Tsk, tsk.* But here's some advice for free:

In the future, jump sparingly.

Head to 242 ●●●

"All right, Space Pirates, time for action," you hear Sgt. Brixto say over the open channel. "They're coming in hot from nine and twelve o'clock. Fly accordingly!"

What do you do?

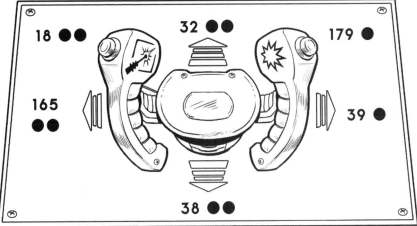

18 ●●

32 ●●

179 ●

165
●●

39 ●

38 ●●

● ●

You press the button that deploys your laser weapon, and it fires a volley of colorful death out into space, but you hit nothing. "Wait until you've got them in your targeting reticle, THEN fire!" you hear Sgt. Brixto say. *Targeting reticle?* you wonder.

Head back to 129 ●

● ● ●

You pull off a shot at the fleeing fighter, but it's quicker than you anticipated, and your shots fly wild. You have to keep up the pursuit and wait until the right moment to shoot. Keep flying!

Head back to 23 ●

● ● ● ●

Retreating to escape from the fireball, you remember too late what you were fleeing and end up running directly into the quick-spreading fire from the ballroom. You are stuck between a spell and a hard place and, well, you get roasted.

Head to 242 ● ● ●

●

Sword practice! Awesome! Other than that, that has no effect here. Choose again.

Head back to 115 ●

●●

You jump as one of the Hortiskull's tendrils waves toward you, evading its grasp neatly. Excellent work! But besides that, nothing happens. The Hortiskull doesn't press an attack. Try a new tactic.

Head back to 136 ●●

●●●

Hoping to avoid the path of destruction, you move to the side of the gate, but unfortunately the ground there isn't stable anymore. It breaks apart, and it's . . . the end.

Head to 242 ●●●

● ● ● ●

The Death-King chases you back, and you move swiftly, remembering at the last moment to leap over the holes in the floor of the throne room that drop away into nothingness. You've bought yourself a moment, but what do you do NOW? Pick a different action!

Head back to 138 ● ● ● ●

●

You turn the control yoke to the left, and your craft banks port . . . directly into the wing of the craft flying next to you! You can hear a curse over the comms system as the other pilot moves away, and then you can hear Sgt. Brixto say, "Hey, are you SURE you're ready for this?"

Head back to 129 ●

● ●

"I will NOT be defeated!" the Death-King cries. "I shall be victorious!" But the Death-King's boasts ring a little hollow. It looks weakened and weathered, and it has raised an arm as if to defend against your next attack! And is that doubt that you hear in the creature's sepulchral voice? A bit of fear, perhaps? Could it be that you've got the nefarious necromancer on the ropes?

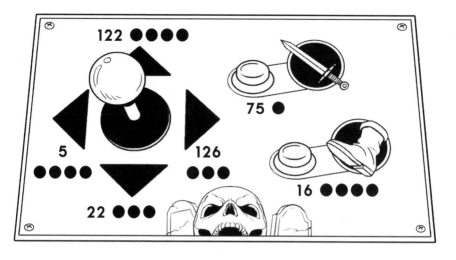

●●●

You move to the left and feel the fireball pass you,
but strangely, there's no heat coming from it—it was
an illusion! It roars down the hall and explodes into
nothingness. But the delay has cost you, for the corridor
the Death-King went down is now sealed, and the fire
from the ballroom has caught up to you!

Head to 242 ●●●

●●●●

You try to push open the wooden gate and move down
the right lane, but no amount of pushing will open it. It
seems as if something—or someONE—doesn't want you
to go this way. Not yet.

Head back to 188 ●

●

You pull up . . . and it's the wrong move! The Galactic
Authority fighter has zigged where you have zagged, and
you've lost them!

Head back to 23 ●

●●

You move toward the toys, and they tilt their heads
slightly, but otherwise remain motionless. They seem to
be waiting for you to do something else. Choose again.

Head back to 64 ●●

●●●

You slowly retreat from the Death-King, hoping to gain
a few moments of rest so you can think about your next
move, but as you step backward, your heel catches
on a stone and you fall through a gaping hole in the
ground! Your arms windmill wildly, but it's too late—you
can't stop your momentum, and down you go, down,
down, down into oblivion. Next time be a little bit more
proactive, eh?

Head to 242 ●●●

●●●●

Seriously? You've got the Black Angel in your crosshairs and you blow it breaking off in another direction? Have you ever heard the phrase "Snatching defeat from the jaws of victory"? Well, you have now! You probably deserve what happens next, which is piloting your ship directly into a hail of enemy fire. Alas!

YOU ARE DEAD. CONTINUE: Y/N?
Y: Head to 43 ●●● **N:** Head to 242 ●●●

●

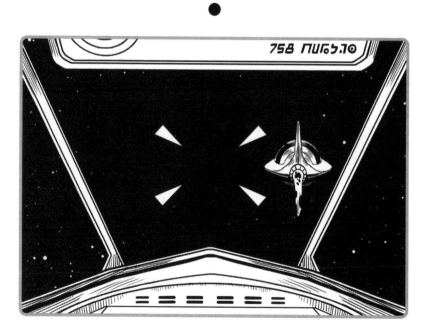

You're still in hot pursuit of your quarry, even though

they're doing everything they can to shake you. What do you do now?

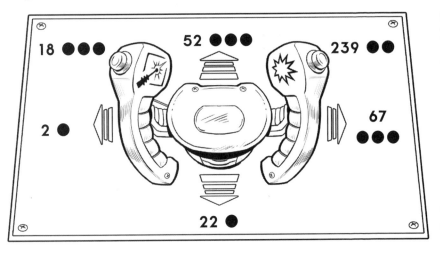

●●

You push forward on your control yoke, and the nose of your space fighter begins to dip, causing you to begin to drift "down" in the void of space, until you feel an impact shake your craft—you've collided with another space fighter in your formation! You pull up and mutter an apology over your comms link.

"Slow down there, Cadet," you hear Sgt. Brixto say. "You'll get a chance to fight soon enough."

Head back to 129 ●

• • •

Figuring that stairs are a good sign, you move C.O.B. to the right and begin your ascent. You climb and climb and climb . . . and then come to a dead end! What? Who builds a stairway to nowhere in the middle of a Slaystation? That's just sloppy design work. As you curse whoever the low bidder was on building this strange place, the Spider-Bots overwhelm C.O.B. and deactivate him with extreme prejudice. Hey—it's their job, but that doesn't mean that you have to enjoy the fact that it's the end.

Head to 242 • • •

• • • •

Remembering a similar standoff from an old movie, and thinking that it might not be able to dodge a blast at such close range, you take advantage of the Gorillosaur's preening display of might and quickly squeeze off a couple of laser blasts, which catch it midhowl! The creature looks at you in surprise and then falls backward, dead!

Head to 145 • •

●

Perhaps you're a little bit twitchy, but you steer your
fighter to the left, away from the ship you're hunting and
directly into the cross fire between another Space Pirates
ship and a Galactic Authority fighter. Smooth move,
Cadet . . .

YOU ARE DEAD. CONTINUE: Y/N?
Y: Head to 129 ● N: Head to 242 ●●●

●●

You jump up and down, and the Death-King stops and
shakes its head. "This is very amusing," it says, "but I
don't have the time for your strange calisthenics." It claps
its hands together, and a wave of dark energy courses
toward you, sending you reeling into a wall, after which
you slide down to the floor, unable to move. The Death-
King moves toward you, and the last thing you see is its
bony hand reaching out toward your face . . .

Head to 242 ●●●

● ● ●

You pull up, and as you do, you hear the angry voice of Sgt. Brixto come in over the comms link. "What do you think you're DOING, Cadet? You had 'em in your sights, and you let 'em get away! Don't let it happen next time!"

Head back to 179 ●

● ● ● ●

You move to the left, hoping to buy yourself a little time. But that choice turns out to be unwise, for as you move, the ground of the throne room cracks and crumbles into nothingness, and you TRIP and fall down into the endless emptiness . . .

Head to 242 ● ● ●

●

You press the button for your special weapon, hoping that somehow, someway, it'll work this time, but it doesn't, of course, and the Black Angel continues its dance just ahead of you, moving erratically, trying to shake you. Try something else!

Head back to 235 ● ● ● ●

● ●

The jungle is completely impassable in every direction but forward, and that way is blocked by the Galactic Authority's hover tank, and each way you move, the cannon tracks you implacably. There's no way out other than THROUGH it.

Try another move!

Head back to 234 ● ● ●

● ● ●

You approach the frozen gate of the Castle-Crypt, the Flame Key in your hand. At your approach, the heat from the key starts to rapidly melt the ice that encases the gate and the lock, and as you place the key in the lock, steam begins to rise. You turn the key and . . . *BOOM!* The gates explode outward, bending as if they've been rent by some magical force. You're thrown backward by the blast and momentarily stunned. When you look up, the gates are mangled and twisted, the lock melted and fused into one solid hunk with the Flame Key, its magic spent and its fire now extinguished.

Beyond the gate, there is a stone bridge, perhaps one hundred yards long, that leads to the entrance of the Castle-Crypt. There are no walls or barriers on either

side of the bridge, and beyond the edges you can see nothing but an abyss. *This is NOT very welcoming*, you think, but it's not like you have a choice. This is the final level, and if you have any hope of getting out of *Crypt Quest*, it lies somewhere inside that castle.

You cross the threshold of the gate. As you do, a ghostly image appears before you—once again, it's the mysterious hooded figure: the strange necromancer, the FINAL BOSS!

"So, you have defeated Skele-King and Stone-King!" it says. "Well done! But if you want to escape my clutches, you must still face ME, the Death-King, in battle. Enter my Castle-Crypt . . . AND DIE!"

The Death-King laughs derisively and disappears into vapor, and then . . . nothing. All is quiet . . . too quiet. The calm lasts for only a moment, because the earth begins to shake, and the ground behind you starts to fall away, leaving NOTHING behind!

The ground behind you is crumbling, and before you is the Castle-Crypt. What do you do?

33 ●●●●

91 ●

19 ●●●

184 ●●●●

46 ●●

40 ●●

●●●●

The jungle is completely impassable in every direction but forward, and that way is blocked by the Galactic Authority's hover tank, and each way you move, the cannon tracks you implacably. There's no way out other than THROUGH it.

Try another move!

Head back to 234 ●●●

●

This time, instead of running, you move slowwwwwly to the left. The Stone-King slowwwwwly turns its head to follow your progress.

"You're just making it mad," says the voice from the Almost-Bottomless Well. "Tsk, tsk, tsk."

You move back to where you were standing before—slowwwwwly—and make another move.

Head back to 110 ●●●

●●

You jam the control yoke forward, and your space fighter dives, just evading a laser strafe from a Galactic Authority fighter. You're still alive . . . for now.

Head back to 129 ●

●●●

Thinking that, like the Skele-King before, the key (no pun intended) to success here is to get behind this boss, you make a run for the space between the Stone-King's legs. But as you do, the Stone-King simply SITS DOWN on you and, well . . .

YOU ARE DEAD. CONTINUE: Y/N?
Y: Head to 196 ●● N: Head to 242 ●●●

●●●●

You move forward, and as you do, the ground directly behind you crumbles, leaving nothing but a void under your heels! Barely gaining purchase in time, you pump your legs as fast as they can move, and even though you are running faster than you've ever run before, you just barely make it to the open doors of the castle before the final brick of the bridge falls away into nothing. In the distance you can still see the graveyard, but there's no way to reach it. You have no choice: You must enter the Castle-Crypt!

Head to 222 ●●

●

You pull the Gorillosaur to the side, hoping to knock it off
balance, but the agile jungle beast rolls with your motion
and FLIPS you over, causing you to crash to the ground.
Before you can recover from the jarring reversal, the
beast stands over you, places both feet squarely on your
body, and TEARS an arm from your Walker! Holding
the arm aloft victoriously, it then brings it down . . . and
connects, through some strange twist of science-fate,
with a circuit inside of your Walker, causing it to blow
sky-high, taking the Gorillosaur (who probably died
happy) with it.

YOU ARE DEAD. CONTINUE: Y/N?
Y: Head to 68 ●●●● N: Head to 242 ●●●

●●

You shoot your lasers at Slaystation Omega, throwing
everything you have at the monstrous space behemoth.
You're joined in this assault by dozens of other Space
Pirates fighters, and each one of you unleashes wave
after wave of laser death upon your target, but nothing
has any effect. With one last battle cry, you pilot your
ship directly toward the Slaystation, hoping that you'll
buy your fellow pilots some time, and as you fire another

volley of lasers, the baleful eyes of the gigantic murder-
base fall upon you, and you are turned into star vapor.

Head to 242 ●●●

●●●

You pull your ship to the right, hoping that maybe, just
maybe, you'll catch the Black Angel doing something
unpredictable. But the only thing here you didn't predict
is the squadron of Galactic Authority fighters you're
piloting your ship directly toward. They shoot, you shoot,
but they shoot more, and that, as they say, is that.

YOU ARE DEAD. CONTINUE: Y/N?
Y: Head to 43 ●●● **N: Head to 242** ●●●

●●●●

Your ship shifts to the right, creaking and groaning as its
engines try to power up enough to achieve liftoff, and for
a moment it seems as if you're going to make it . . . but
then the engines begin to whine and sputter, and your
ship starts to spin wildly out of control toward the hover
tank! The Galactic Authority troops scatter as you collide
and . . .

YOU ARE DEAD. CONTINUE: Y/N?
Y: Head to 56 ●● **N: Head to 242** ●●●

●

The Death-King snaps its fingers, and the stones of the throne room floor fall away, revealing an endless void below. But fortunately you retreat at just the right moment and stumble backward, falling down but still managing to avoid the bottomless pit. As you scramble backward, your hand touches something familiar—it's your sword! Your fingers wrap around the grip of the blade, and you climb to your feet, once again armed and ready for action!

Continue to 138 ●●●●

●●

You turn the control yoke to the right, slowly edging toward the fighter flying directly to starboard. A burst of alien language comes over your comms unit, and even though you don't understand the strange words, you can tell they're angry ones aimed at you. Mumbling an apology, you gently correct your course to head straight toward the enemy fighters.

Head back to 129 ●

●●●

You punch the air around you, feeling ready for action, but there's nothing around for you to punch. Your battles will begin soon, but there is something else you must do first. Think again.

Head back to 167 ●

●●●●

You ARE aware that this place has the words "Certain" and "Doom" carved above its door, right? And you're okay with that? Okay, you're braver than we thought. By all means, enter . . .

Head to 87 ●●●

●

As the Gorillosaur runs forward, you make your Walker mech take a few cautious steps back, trotting just out of range of your foe's grasping claws. The Gorillosaur then warily falls back, and you and it begin circling each other, each trying to plan out a devastating attack.

Choose another action!

Head back to 68 ●●●●

You pull back on the control yoke . . . and realize too late that when Sgt. Brixto said twelve o'clock, he was referring to up, the direction you're now going in. As the lasers of the Galactic Authority fighter turn your ship into a ball of space debris, all you can think is, *Whoops*.

YOU ARE DEAD. CONTINUE: Y/N?
Y: Head to 129 ● **N:** Head to 242 ●●

●●●

You move to the left, and the chattering skull HOPS into the air, its jaw *clitter-clack*ing open and closed quickly. Before you can raise your hands to defend yourself, it CHOMPS YOU RIGHT IN THE FACE. The bad news? You're dead. The good news? You get another chance.

YOU ARE DEAD. CONTINUE: Y/N?
Y: Head to 167 ● **N:** Head to 242 ●●●

●●●●

You pump your fists at the skeleton and connect only with air, as you don't want your hands to get too close to the grasping creature. Punching this thing again just isn't going to work. Sorry.

Head back to 193 ●●●●

●

With a *whoosh*, you narrowly avoid the laser beams from a Galactic Authority fighter. Now to keep doing that over and over and over . . . or take the fight TO them!

Head back to 129 ●

●●

The jungle is completely impassable in every direction but forward, and that way is blocked by the Galactic Authority's hover tank, and each way you move, the cannon tracks you implacably. There's no way out other than THROUGH it.

Try another move!

Head back to 234 ●●●

●●●

You roll to your right, stopping just short of falling down into the void the Death-King made with its last volley of attacks, but as you do, the Death-King creeps even closer to you. Try a different move!

Head back to 138 ●●●●

●●●●

You move toward the reanimated skeleton and swiftly realize that you've made a mistake. It moves quickly in your direction, like an insect made out of magic and bone, and gets so close that you can't even bring your hands up to defend yourself before its bony claws grab you around the neck, drawing blood. Pushing it away, you realize that you have to try something else.

Head back to 184 ●

●

As you press this button, you hear an annoying buzzing noise in your cockpit, but that's it. Nothing else happens. "Forget that button for now, Cadet," you hear Sgt. Brixto say. "Now's not the time. Eyes forward."

Head to 17 ●

●●

You leap just ahead of the crumbling ground, landing on solid brick, then jump again, and again, and again. Moments later, you are safely standing just inside the entrance to the Castle-Crypt. Behind you, the bridge has disappeared. The only way out is IN.

Head to 222 ●●

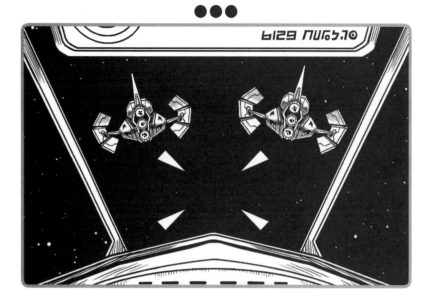

There are now TWO Black Angels. The fiend must be using some sort of tactical cloaking/illusion device! One Black Angel is to the left of your targeting guide, and the other is to the right. Which one will you chase?

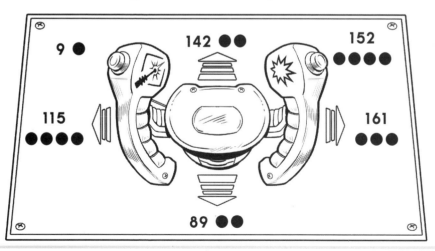

●●●●

Reacting almost instinctively, you push down on your control yoke and dive. The Black Angel wasn't ready for your style of reckless, nonsensical piloting, and shoots past you. Taking advantage of your enemy's miscalculation, you quickly pull up and find yourself directly behind the dreaded pilot. Nice one!

Head to 235 ●●●●

●

You begin to backtrack away from the Hortiskull, and as you do, it gathers its body against the gate, as if to guard it. But it's not attacking, just . . . waiting, as if it knows that you're not ready to face it. A moment passes, then the creature shifts its body, slipping through the bars of the gate and disappearing away into the swamp. Knowing when to give up, you hustle back down toward the crossroads of the graveyard.

Head back to 162 ●

●●

Mysteriously, you decide that NOW is the time to unleash C.O.B.'s weapon. Why you'd want to do that BEFORE the cute li'l' bot has reached his goal, we have no idea. But, hey—if that's your choice, C.O.B. will abide by it, and abide by it the robot does. As he activates his bomb, destroying both him and the Spider-Bots that are after him (but, sadly, not the rest of the Slaystation), you derive little satisfaction knowing that after all you've been through, it's now the end.

Head to 242 ●●●

●●●

The readouts and technical diagrams have once again appeared on your screen, and you can tell instantly that something is wrong, for everything is flashing RED, and behind the small dot on your screen that represents your fighter there's another dot, and it's GAINING on you. Whatever it is, this dot looks like it means business. Bad business.

"If you're wondering what that is coming up on your six, well, I'm not gonna lie to you. That there is the Black Angel, the meanest ace pilot that the Galactic Authority has. Intelligence told us that the Black Angel was fighting somewhere else, but it looks like intelligence wasn't so, uh, intelligent. Sorry about tha*KKKKKZKKKZZZZZT!*"

Static fills your screen, cutting off Sgt. Brixto. After a moment, the static is replaced by a new image, that of another pilot. But this pilot isn't wearing the uniform of a Space Pirate. Instead, it's wearing a dark helmet and looks like some sort of ferocious monster.

"Greetings, Cadet," the Black Angel says, its scratchy, evil voice sending a shiver down your spine. "How does it feel to be the next mark on my kill list? Ha ha ha ha! Don't worry—I promise to make this quick! Here's a small taste of what's to come!"

Suddenly a blast rocks your space fighter. The Black

Angel has fired the first shot! Then, to add insult to injury, the Black Angel's craft zooms past yours and wags its wings, almost as if it is daring you to fight back. And you know that you have no choice—this is a battle you must win . . . or die trying!

The Black Angel is flying in front of you, weaving back and forth so you can't get a fix on its position, when suddenly, it slows DOWN and you speed past it. All that fancy flying was a trick to distract you, and now, once again, you're the one being hunted. What do you do?

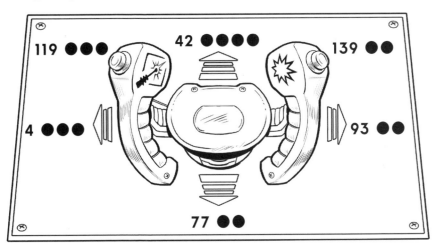

119 ●●●   42 ●●●●   139 ●●

4 ●●●   93 ●●

77 ●●

●●●●

BRZAAAP! BRZAAAP! With the Galactic Authority craft dead in your sights, you shoot your lasers and . . . the ship explodes in a spectacular fireball. It's a direct hit! Yesssssss!

"Excellent shot, Cadet!" you hear Sgt. Brixto say. "I was sure you were a goner, but even ol' Sgt. Brixto gets it wrong every once in a while. But hey—are you gonna just sit there and pat yourself on the back, or are you gonna join the rest of us fighting this Space Battle?"

Head to 100 ●●●

●

Even though you no longer have a sword, you realize that you're not powerless—you still hold the Flame Key in your hand, and you know that it contains some sort of great magic. In a last-ditch effort, you decide to find out, and, clutching it so that its teeth stick out from your clenched fist, you PUNCH THE STONE-KING WITH THE FLAME KEY.

Head to 127 ●●●●

●●

Ordinarily, your sword is very useful when you're in a jam, but not now. You swing it, but it's a futile gesture, and the wasted moment was a moment you didn't have to waste. You did not choose wisely! The ground crumbles beneath you, and it's . . . the end.

Head to 242 ●●●

●●●

Pulling your ship to the right, you realize too late that the Galactic Authority fighter is pulling to its LEFT. Two wrongs don't make a right, and two rights don't make a wrong, but a left and a right make, at least in this instance, a head-on collision in the vacuum of space. And for you, that means that . . .

YOU ARE DEAD. CONTINUE: Y/N?
Y: Head to 129 ● **N:** Head to 242 ●●●

●●●●

Your ship lurches to the left . . . and crashes directly into a tree, causing it to crack and then fall onto your ship! Sparks fly from your control panel, and in moments, Galactic Authority troops have surrounded your ship, their weapons trained on you! Try something else!

Head back to 56 ●●

●

Hoping to collect your thoughts in safety, you begin to bound down the stairs on the right. But as you do, you hear a rumble behind. Sparing a moment to glance backward, you see an avalanche of rubble following you! Surprised, you trip, fall, and are immediately overtaken by the wave of waste.

YOU ARE DEAD. CONTINUE: Y/N?
Y: Head to 196 ●● N: Head to 242 ●●●

●●

The Walker clumsily moves to the side as the Galactic Authority hover tank trains its cannon on you, shooting an energy blast that narrowly misses you. Whether it was by accident or design, you've avoided getting a faceful of laser. Choose another action!

Head back to 166 ●●●●

●●●

Aside from being a running bomb, C.O.B. is completely unarmed. Try something else!

Head back to 105 ●●

You jump up and grab on to the Skele-King, getting a good grip in its rib cage. It tries to swat you off its back, but it can't, and you barely make it onto its shoulders. Barely, but still!

What do you do?

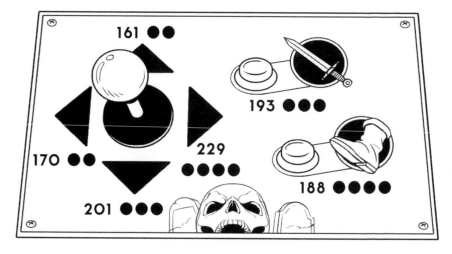

The enchanted toys at first seem amused at your japing jumps and mimic you, hopping up and down on their wooden legs. But they're hopping closer, and closer, and closer, and then . . . they all jump on YOU! Who knew that wooden teeth could be so sharp?

YOU ARE DEAD. CONTINUE: Y/N?
Y: Head to 188 ● **N:** Head to 242 ●●●

●●

Sorry, there's no going back! Choose again.
Head back to 105 ●●

●●●

Using those catlike reflexes you've honed over the previous levels, you juke to the left and just barely avoid the Death-King's death-dealing death ray, which instead kills a decent-size section of the stone floor of the throne room. But there's no time to gloat, for the Death-King looks ready to attack again! Choose another tactic.

Head back to 216 ●●●

●●●●

Nope. Nothing. What is WITH this thing, anyway?

Head back to 69 ●

●

You try to feint to the right, but the Skele-King brings down its enormous broadsword, forcing you to reconsider.

Head back to 206 ●●●

●●

You try to head north, but the vines that lie across the path come to sinuous life, blocking you from going in that direction. Try a different way.

Head back to 136 ●●

● ● ●

You put your space fighter into a dive (well, a "dive"—this is outer space, so it's all relative) in the hopes of keeping up with the Galactic Authority fighter, but it flies to the right and out of range. You've got to find it again before IT finds YOU!

Head back to 23 ●

● ● ● ●

Look: We understand. Fleeing for your life is a legitimate decision when you're in a life-threatening situation. But this is not the time or place for running away. This isn't real life; this is a VIDEO GAME. And you've got this.

Head back to 110 ● ● ●

●

Hoping to gain a little bit of time, you make your Walker take a step back. Sadly, the thick jungle blocks your retreat. You can't go this way! Choose again.

Head back to 166 ● ● ● ●

● ●

You press forward, following the fleeing Death-King, and as you do, the chandeliers above you begin to fall—*CRASH! CRASH! CRASH!*—each one landing and exploding into flames. You can feel the heat as their fire begins to consume the hall behind you and starts to chase you. There's no going back now.

Head to 74 ● ● ● ●

● ● ●

You fire your weapons at the Gorillosaur, but the beast is, despite its size, incredibly nimble, and it dodges every blast, hopping from side to side but continuing forward until it leaps upon you! You've barely got enough time to raise your arms in defense, and now you and the Gorillosaur are grappling!

Head to 218 ● ● ● ●

● ● ● ●

As he runs, C.O.B. raises a hand, extends his index finger, cocks his thumb, and pretends to shoot a laser gun. It's pretty cute, but yes, he's only pretending because he's unarmed! Choose again.

Head back to 4 ● ●

●

You try to move eastward, but a crumbling wall from a sarcophagus blocks your way and won't let you go any farther, as if there is something else you must accomplish before you can embark upon your Crypt Quest. Choose again.

Head back to 167 ●

●●

You lunge to the left, hoping to dash down the path there and perhaps make it to the Village Gate, but with a gesture the Abominable Snowmancer wills a wall of ice and snow to form in front of you, blocking your escape. You turn and try to go in another direction, but it's too late. The creature first touches your upraised sword with its hand, causing the blade to freeze and shatter. Then, seeing that you're defenseless, it opens its mouth and breathes a cone of frozen air toward you, freezing you mid-flee in moments.

YOU ARE DEAD. CONTINUE: Y/N?
Y: Head to 167 ● **N: Head to 242** ●●●

●●●

With the reticle lit, you figure that if there is any time that your special weapon will work, it will be now. Crossing your fingers, you press the button . . . and *FWOOSH*! A missile takes flight from your ship, heading straight toward the Black Angel. The enemy ship weaves to and fro, attempting to avoid being struck, but the missile continues on, getting closer . . . closer . . . closer . . . then *BOOM*! It connects with the Black Angel's ship, vaporizing it. And like the completely awesome Space Pirate you are, you fly THROUGH the debris in a spectacular show of coolness.

Head to 123 ●

●●●●

Moving in this direction was your first—and last— mistake, for you've piloted your Walker into a newly formed chasm in the floor of the jungle. As you plummet, your Walker collides with and scrapes against the sides of the hole you're falling down, and you try to grasp hold of anything that will arrest your momentum, but nothing works. There's no doubt about it . . .

YOU ARE DEAD. CONTINUE: Y/N?
Y: Head to 56 ●● **N: Head to 242** ●●●

●

For some unfathomable reason, you move TOWARD the Abominable Snowmancer, perhaps hoping to tackle it or hug it to death. Unfortunately, whatever your reasoning, it's a terrible decision. Seeing an opportunity, the creature first touches your upraised sword with its hand, causing the blade to freeze and shatter. Then, seeing that you're defenseless, it wraps its arms around YOU. The effect is immediate. Your body is almost instantaneously frozen solid, and YOU HAVE BEEN HUGGED TO DEATH.

YOU ARE DEAD. CONTINUE: Y/N?
Y: Head to 167 ● N: Head to 242 ●●●

●●

Everything is dark.

And all is quiet.

But actually, not really . . .

In the darkness, you can hear white noise . . .

Perhaps it's just your ears ringing from the crash.

Realizing that your eyes are closed, you open them slowly.

You're still strapped in to the seat of your space fighter. The airbag has deflated, and looking out of the cockpit, you can see that your ship has come to rest on the floor of the thick jungle that you crashed through . . . how long ago? Seconds, minutes . . . hours, maybe. And that noise you're hearing? It's the deafening sound of everything alive in this jungle doing its thing.

You think back for a minute to your friends. You wonder if they are still waiting for you or wondering what is taking you so long. But soon, you come back to the present, as you have no other choice.

Shaking your head groggily, you look around the cockpit, your eyes fixing upon the computer display that's been giving you your information, hoping that you'll see the ornery face of Sgt. Brixto pop up on it.

No luck.

The display is dead.

You hit it twice with the side of your fist, not expecting much, but to your surprise, it lights up. At first, it displays nothing but garbled gibberish, and you fear the worst—it's broken, and you're marooned on this weird planet. But after a few moments, the display resets and displays this message:

Phew. You're still in the game, still trapped somewhere in the Midnight Arcade. But what challenges will this new level and new world present, and how will you eventually beat the game and get out? You're stuck on an alien jungle planet in what appears to be a busted spaceship, so whatever it is, you know that it's going to be TOUGH.

You press a few buttons in the cockpit and try to move the control yoke around, but nothing responds. The only thing that happens when you try to get anything to work is that a neutral computer voice announces, "Internal repair in progress."

Pressing up on the canopy, you manage to shove it open, and crawling down from the cockpit, you find yourself standing on the jungle floor. The sound of the local fauna is now almost deafening; everything is buzzing, hooting, squonking, bleating, and crying. Walking around your space fighter cautiously, senses alert for anything out of the ordinary, you inspect the damage. Scorch marks decorate the hull of the ship, giving it an admittedly cool patina of battle scarring. But it also looks like it's partially broken; things look out of place, as if they were somehow shifted in the crash landing, and it doesn't look good.

And that's when you notice that the sounds of the jungle have stopped. It's now completely silent . . . until there's a new sound, a distinctive HUM of technology, followed by the unmistakable crack and crash of trees being felled. Looking behind you, through the trees, you can see its source—a hovering TANK is making its way through the greenery, toward you, a tank that looks a LOT like the Galactic Authority fighters you were just vaporizing. It's being led by soldiers on foot, one of whom points in your direction. At that, the other soldiers raise their laser guns and begin shooting toward you as the hover tank charges forward toward your position.

Quickly you climb back up into the cockpit of your
space fighter and close the canopy, and as you do, a bell
dings, and the computer voice chimes in again.

"Repair complete. Walker mode now available."
Walker mode? Was that what Sgt. Brixto mentioned? The
engines of your vehicle hum as they come to life. You're
back online and ready for action, apparently.

What do you do?

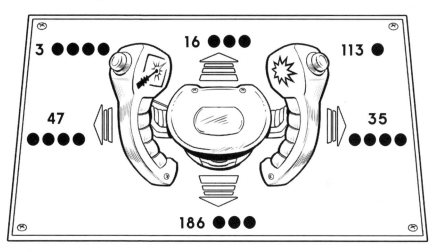

Following the trail of the noxious necromancer through the labyrinth of the castle, you come to another crossroads . . . and are confronted by a terrifying TRIO of Death-Kings! "There are three of me before you, but only one is real! Make the wrong choice . . . AND DIE!"

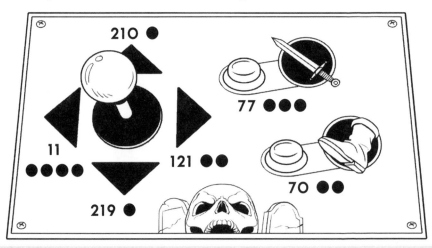

●●●●

Your targeting guide has lit up; the Slaystation, as huge as it is, is DIRECTLY in your sights. *Here goes nothing*, you say to yourself as you press your special weapon button, fully expecting nothing to happen. So you're surprised that when you press it, at least a dozen missiles leap from your ship, dancing and weaving their way toward the Slaystation. Closer . . . closer . . . closer . . . It's a direct hit! The surface of the Slaystation erupts with explosive blossoms as each of your missiles detonates . . . to no discernible effect whatsoever. The Slaystation is completely unharmed! Although some might take issue with this definition, we'd classify "special weapon doesn't work well then works really well but does nothing" as being pretty ironic.

And as that amazed thought goes through your head, your ship is raked by fire from an enemy ship, and you are turned into non-ironic space debris.

Head to 242 ●●●

●

Entering Ye Olde Provisions Shoppe, you are greeted by the sight of something you certainly NEVER expected to see anywhere in *Crypt Quest*: a soda machine?!

It hums with life, even though it doesn't appear to actually be plugged in to any power source. Perplexed, you approach the machine. Thirsty, you press one of its buttons. The machine buzzes and . . .

CH-CHUNK! A can of Midnight Cola falls into the opening below. You grab it, and you're surprised at how nice and cold it is. You pull the tab—*PSSHT!*—and, figuring that you have nothing to lose, chug the soda.

It's the most delicious soda you've ever had in your LIFE. And as you drink it, you hear a noise from far off . . . that sounds like the other wooden gate in the plaza opening! Awesome!

Completely refreshed, you exit Ye Olde Provisions Shoppe and head back to the plaza.

Head to 201 ●●●●

●●

Inside Ye Olde Toy Shoppe, you find yourself in a dusty room lined with shelves and more shelves, and each shelf is groaning under the weight of TOYS. There are wooden goblin puppets on one shelf, each with a terrible, lifelike grin painted on its gnarled face. On another shelf there are carved wooden dragons with clockwork keys in their sides, ready to be wound up.

There are hundreds of toys in the shop, and one thing they all have in common is that they look BAD. Not badly made—no, whoever crafted them was obviously very skilled. But their maker was also obviously demented and, perhaps, a little on the nefarious side. There's some sinister magic afoot in this place, and the toys seem to be the focus of it.

So: It seems as if you've stepped into a room of creepy, enchanted wooden toys. What do you do?

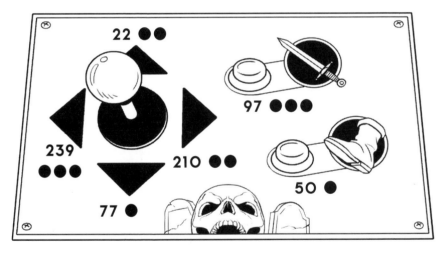

You try to move, but the Gorillosaur anticipates your motion and swiftly jumps on you, this time using its agility to flip over you and grab you from behind. You frantically try to shake the beast off, but it's holding on

tight, its jaws snapping at the head of the Walker. Then
it climbs up to your Walker's shoulders, grabs its head
(which houses your cockpit, of course), and RIPS IT OFF
and throws it aside. You watch helplessly as you hurtle
through the air. The Gorillosaur stands over the fallen
body of the Walker mech, beating its chest victoriously.
Then, its celebration finished, it turns toward you and
walks over. Kneeling down, it peers into the cockpit,
sniffing at it with curiosity. Then once again it howls, and
that's when you know that . . .

YOU ARE DEAD. CONTINUE: Y/N?
Y: Head to 68 ●●●● N: Head to 242 ●●●

●●●●

You back away from the Abominable Snowmancer,
and as you do, it raises its arms in an ominous motion.
The sound of ice cracking and forming fills the air, and
a moment later, when you back into a wall that wasn't
there before, you realize that the creature just magically
formed a barrier of solid ice to bar your escape. The
Abominable Snowmancer rushes toward you, and you
raise your sword to defend yourself, but it's no use. It
grabs the blade, causing it to freeze and shatter. And then
it grabs YOU. Before you can say "I prefer ice cream,"

you are turned into an adventurer popsicle and . . .

YOU ARE DEAD. CONTINUE: Y/N?
Y: Head to 167 ● N: Head to 242 ●●●

●

You try to move northward, but an impenetrable green fog springs up before you, and you can't see to proceed. It's almost as if there is something else you must do first, before you begin the Crypt Quest. Try something else.

Head back to 167 ●

●●

You try to jump again, but this time the Stone-King has become wise to your wily tricks and swats you backward in midair, forcing you to collide with the gate to the plaza.

YOU ARE DEAD. CONTINUE: Y/N?
Y: Head to 196 ●● N: Head to 242 ●●●

●●●

You pull to the right and keep the Galactic Authority fighter in your sights, and it works. You've almost got them. Almost, but not yet. Keep flying!

Head to 232 ●●●

The good news: You're almost off this jungle hellscape of a planet. The bad news: The Gorillosaur wants to make sure you don't do that.

What do you do?

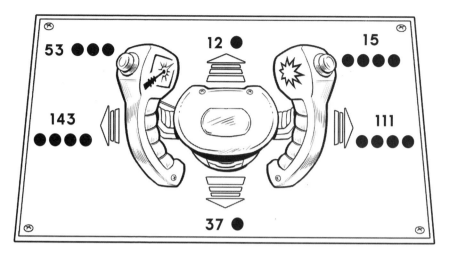

53 ●●●   12 ●   15 ●●●●

143 ●●●●   111 ●●●●

37 ●

●

Another Galactic Authority fighter has crept into view.
The hunt is on—time to rack up some kills!

What do you do?

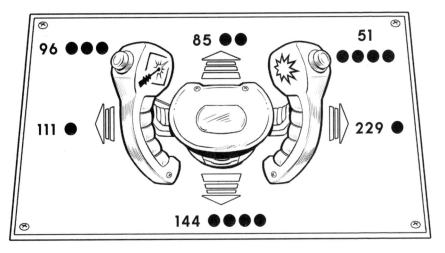

96 ●●●

85 ●●

51 ●●●●

111 ●

229 ●

144 ●●●●

●●

You jump in place, and all three of the Death-Kings before you cackle evilly as they raise their hands together . . . and then *ZZZZAAAPPPP!* Bolts of arcane energy erupt from thirty fingertips all at once, all aimed at you! The magic lightning strikes you in midair, and for a moment you can see your bones through your flesh, almost as if you had just been struck by a very painful supernatural X-ray. The novelty wears off almost immediately, though, as you are dead before you hit the ground.

Head to 242 ●●●

The image on the screen changes, and now you and Sgt. Brixto are looking at the battle raging around Slaystation Omega. The Space Pirates ships are locked in intense dogfights with Galactic Authority ships, and it's a scene of chaos. But something strange is going on. Cracks begin to appear on the surface of Slaystation Omega, cracks from which fiery light spills out. The cracks spread rapidly, and the beams of destruction that were just a moment ago shooting from the eyes of the Slaystation sputter, then stop altogether. In moments, the entirety of the Slaystation is covered with fissures, each one of them oozing light. You could swear that the malevolent expression on the strange face of the Slaystation changes to one of confusion, but that passes instantly, as it is a moment later completely consumed and EXPLODES!

"You did it, Lieutenant!" Sgt. Brixto exclaims, wrapping you in a painful but adoring hug.

You hear an alert noise come from your screen, and the image of the exploding Slaystation is replaced by this:

**CONGRATULATIONS!
YOU HAVE BEEN
PROMOTED TO THE
RANK OF SPACE
PIRATE CAPTAIN!**

"You might be the single greatest Space Pirate to ever pirate space," Sgt. Brixto says. "C'mon. Let's go down to the hangar and see what's happening down there."

Exiting the torpedo bay, you and Brixto make your way through the mazelike corridors of the Space Pirates ship, finally emerging into the vast hangar bay where you began your adventure. Hundreds of your fellow Space Pirates are gathered there, attending to the fighter ships that are landing in the bay, some of them extremely battle-scarred. When you enter, a hush falls over the crowd.

And then, the Space Pirates begin to cheer. They're cheering for YOU. And it's at that moment that you know you've accomplished the next-to-impossible.

You've beaten *Space Battles*.

You walk away from the celebration, accepting hearty pats on the back, and head toward the end of the hangar, which looks out upon the vastness of space. The wreckage of Slaystation Omega floats there, its fearsomeness reduced to trash for space scavengers. As you take in the strange beauty of the place you're in, your thoughts are interrupted by the arrival of Sgt. Brixto, who stands next to you and speaks.

"So, Captain," Sgt. Brixto says. "Seems like you've got quite the career ahead of you with the Space Pirates. Whattaya think you'll do now? And do you think you could see your way to maybe taking ol' Brixto along on any future adventures you might have?"

You turn to the sergeant and extend your hand. He takes it and gives it a mighty shake, and it's clear to you now that your time with the Space Pirates is over and you can leave the game. So what do you do?

If you want to play *Crypt Quest* now, head to 167 ●

If you want to finish your session at the Midnight Arcade, head to 242 ●●●

●●●●

The Death-King turns to face you and moves its hands in a rapid and complicated series of motions, and as it does, its bony claws begin to glow brightly. Flames form around its hands, coalescing into a bright sphere of fire! For a moment the magic fireball hangs there in the air, but then the Death-King winds up like a pitcher in a baseball game and THROWS the fireball, aiming it directly at you!

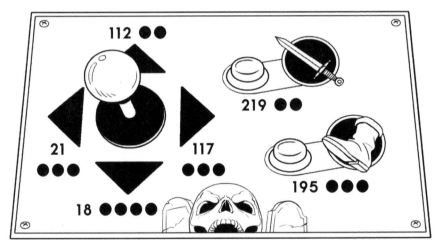

●

Seizing the opportunity, you charge at the stunned
Death-King, and with both hands you jam your sword
at the monster . . . and your blow lands! Your sword
pierces the Death-King's bony chest, and you look at
your opponent with shock, and it looks back at you with
horrified acknowledgment of what just happened. Could
this be the END?!

Head to 6 ●●●

●●

You press the special weapon button, and if you were
hoping for a miracle of some sort, you are sorely
disappointed. Nothing happens . . . except for the hover
tank taking advantage of you wasting time by firing its
cannon directly at you.

YOU ARE DEAD. CONTINUE: Y/N?
Y: Head to 56 ●● **N: Head to 242** ●●●

You're standing at the gate to the graveyard and can move north toward the Crypt Gate, west toward the Village Gate, or east toward the Swamp Gate. So, where to now?

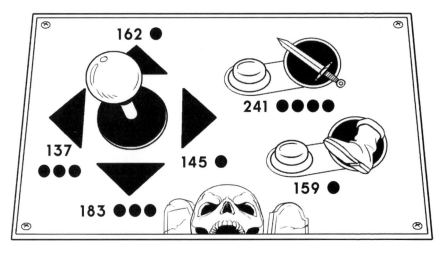

You move backward, and seemingly on instinct, your Walker kneels down and PICKS UP the fallen tree trunk. As it does, the hover tank fires another blast, which passes just over the top of your Walker and blows apart a tree behind you. That was close! But guess what? You're armed now! Well, kind of. Make the most of it.

Head to 234 ●●●

●

Deciding that staying in a room full of animated toys that look as if they want to do very bad things to you is a bad idea, you say, "Excuse me, but I was looking for the arcade," and exit the shop, pulling the door shut behind you.

Head to 115 ●

●●

Reacting almost instinctively, you pull back on your control yoke, pulling your space fighter into a 360-degree loop, which once again puts you on the tail of the Black Angel. Good move!

Head to 235 ●●●●

●●●

Your sword is definitely handy, but it's of no use here. Try again.

Head back to 62 ●●●

●●●●

A couple of hours later, you and a crowd of Space Pirates pilots, mechanics, and other assorted support personnel are gathered in a briefing room aboard the Space Pirates flagship. Word about your exploits has spread around the Space Pirates organization, and you can feel the eyes of your fellow fighters upon you.

Looking about, you catch the sight of some of them giving you a thumbs-up, or a tentacle- or claw-up. Even though YOU know you're trapped in some sort of strange video game, you can't help but feel a little bit of pride. You've made it this far, through a dogfight in outer space and a trek through an alien jungle in a cool mech. What could be next in *Space Battles*?

You imagine some of your friends in uniform around you, knowing they would be as excited as you are to be having this experience. Would they even believe you if you told them about this?

You wonder, too, if they are still outside the abandoned mall worrying about you and wondering why you're taking so long inside.

If they only knew . . .

"All right, Space Pirates! Listen up!" says Sgt. Brixto as he strides into the room. When the assembled crew doesn't immediately stop murmuring, he stops in the center of the room and stands stock-still, his weird eye-patched head moving slowly to let his gaze fall on each being in the room. One by one, everybody stops chattering until, finally, all is silent. A toothy, fang-y smile spreads over the sergeant's face.

"That's more like it," he says. "Good. I'm sure you've all heard by now about our new cadet's, excuse me, corporal's, wait, LIEUTENANT's exploits in that Space Battle, and then their ridiculous story of survival down on the jungle planet, but that's all in the past. What matters now is our final assault on the Galactic Authority's stronghold, their number one base and the seat of their power. If we destroy this place, then it's 'bye-bye' to tyranny and the end of the Space Battles."

"What's the mission, then, Sarge?" asks another Space Pirates pilot.

"I'm glad you asked. Feast your eyes on this beauty," says Sgt. Brixto, pointing to a darkened display screen behind him that blinks on. It reads:

Everybody in the room starts murmuring and talking all at once, reacting to the image.

"Quiet down, quiet down," says the sergeant, continuing. "I'm not saying that it'll be easy, but don't let the name of the thing scare you off. It's half hype, I tell ya—"

BOOM! An explosion interrupts Sgt. Brixto's reassurances, and klaxon warnings begin to sound.

"They've found us sooner than we expected. I thought we had more time, but it looks like this is it, Space Pirates. To your battle stations!"

As the ship rocks and shakes from the impact of the Galactic Authority's strike, the assembled Space Pirates scatter and scramble toward their battle stations. At first you make to do the same, but Sgt. Brixto runs up to you and grabs you by the arm.

"Not so fast, Corporal! I mean, Lieutenant! You've got another mission. Follow me!"

Sgt. Brixto motions for you to follow in a direction that's the exact opposite of where everybody else is going. What's he up to?

If you follow the other Space Pirates, head to 171 ●●●●

If you follow Sgt. Brixto, head to 105 ●●

●

You attempt to move somewhere, anywhere, to avoid the next blast from the hover tank's cannon, but no matter which direction you go, the barrel of its weapon tracks you . . . and then fires! And as it turns out, your Walker can't survive another blast. This one cripples it, causing a complete systems shutdown. The legs on the mech seize up, and the vehicle topples over, with you inside. You black out for a moment, then come to, and when you do, you see Galactic Authority troops surrounding your cockpit, weapons aimed straight at you through the cracked glass. It looks like they're waiting for the command to fire. And then one of them speaks up.

"All right . . . fire!"

And they do. Ouch.

YOU ARE DEAD. CONTINUE: Y/N?
Y: Head to 56 ●● N: Head to 242 ●●●

●●

Any movement you make seems to send an alert to whatever strange intelligence controls the vines, causing them to squeeze your Walker tighter and slither up your body with even more speed. You pull the controls back, push them forward, and yank them to the right and to the left, but the vines continue to move and squeeze, until you are a vine-wrapped Walker mech mummy. Cracks appear in your cockpit's canopy, and the vines put more and more pressure on it, and then . . .

CRASH! The canopy breaks open, and the vines move IN.

YOU ARE DEAD. CONTINUE: Y/N?
Y: Head to 56 ●● N: Head to 242 ●●●

●●●

You hustle to the right, the goal being to stall the Death-King for a few moments until you can figure out a plan of action, but sadly, the Death-King already has a plan figured out, which is to use its magic to cause the ground beneath you to waste away into nothingness. Your feet find no purchase, and you try to move back to where you started, but your effort is futile, and once your body realizes that there's nothing holding you up, gravity takes control . . .

Head to 242 ●●●

●●●●

Figuring that nothing good can come out of going to the right, you decide to guide C.O.B. down the passage to the left, toward the sounds of activity. With the Spider-Bots close behind, you make a break for it. For a few moments, it seems as if everything is A-OK, and C.O.B. puts even more distance between him and the bots after him.

But then . . . you reach the end of the passage and realize too late that the sounds of activity you heard were those of a squad of Galactic Authority troops arming themselves in their barracks, presumably getting ready to raid the Space Pirates base. Seeing C.O.B. and the Spider-Bots behind him, they quickly realize that their new visitor is, in fact, an intruder, and raising their weapons, they reduce C.O.B. to spare parts with amazing efficiency. You were close—SO CLOSE—but now it's the end.

Head to 242 ● ● ●

●

You try to dodge to the left, only to see that the Skele-King's rage has littered your escape path with rubble, making it impassable! Try again.

Head back to 114 ● ●

● ●

Having a hunch where the Galactic Authority ship might be heading, you dive after it . . . and you're right! It continues to try to shake you, though. Stay alert!

Head to 23 ●

• • •

You decide that you don't like the vibe of this spooky cul-
de-sac and choose to promptly head back to the plaza.

Chicken.

Head to 94 • • •

• • • •

In the words of a famous space captain, "Never retreat,
never surrender!" C.O.B. won't go back—his mission is
ahead! Pick another option.

Head back to 4 • •

•

You move the Walker forward, its feet crushing the
foliage beneath you. The Galactic Authority soldiers raise
their weapons and fire, but their shots bounce harmlessly
off the Walker's armor plating. As you advance, the
Galactic Authority troops scatter, but the hover tank
doesn't budge. Instead, it levels its cannon at you . . . and
fires! The beam catches you full in the chest, blowing
you backward into a tree, causing it to break at the base
and fall over. Timber! But incredibly, you're still alive.

Head to 141 • • • •

●●

Thinking you have the element of surprise, you move toward the Death-King . . . and it moves toward you! Before you realize it, the foul creature has wrapped you in its cold embrace. You struggle to free your sword arm, but it's no use—you can feel the necromancer's touch sucking the vitality from your body, draining you of all energy until you turn into a pile of bones and armor.

Head to 242 ●●●

●●●

You enter this shop with morbid curiosity. *Who would name their store Ye Olde Shoppe of Certain Doom? What would they sell?* you ask yourself.

Once you enter, you understand, for you haven't entered a shop so much as a portal to somewhere you definitely DON'T want to go. As you turn to run away, the door to the shop slams shut, and the vacuum from the void starts to drag you in. Grabbing on to the Shoppe's doorknob, you stop your backward momentum . . . but only for a moment, as a tentacle clutches your ankle and pulls you free. As you are dragged toward your fate, you hear the voice of the mysterious villain that has been taunting you since you entered the game:

"What part of 'Ye Olde Certain Doom Shoppe' didn't you understand?! Ha ha ha ha!"

And as it turns out . . .

YOU ARE DEAD. CONTINUE: Y/N?
Y: Head to 188 ●   N: Head to 242 ●●●

●●●●

You try to move, but the Gorillosaur anticipates your motion and swiftly jumps on you, this time using its agility to flip over you and grab you from behind. You frantically try to shake the beast off, but it's holding on tight, its jaws snapping at the head of the Walker. Then it climbs up to your Walker's shoulders, grabs its head (which houses your cockpit, of course), and RIPS IT OFF and throws it aside. You watch helplessly as you hurtle through the air. The Gorillosaur stands over the fallen body of the Walker mech, beating its chest victoriously. Then, its celebration finished, it turns toward you and walks over. Kneeling down, it peers into the cockpit, sniffing at it with curiosity. Then once again it howls, and that's when you know that . . .

YOU ARE DEAD. CONTINUE: Y/N?
Y: Head to 68 ●●●●   N: Head to 242 ●●●

●

You jump, but you do not land, for while you are in the air, the Death-King zaps the floor beneath you, causing it to buckle and tear apart . . . revealing deep, dark EMPTINESS beneath. You throw your hands out and attempt to grab the edge of what's left of the floor, but your fingers find no purchase, and you plummet down into the nothing, closely followed by the Death-King's laughter.

What is it with all this jumping, anyway?

Head to 242 ●●●

●●

Pulling up for some reason, you lose sight of both Black Angels . . . until you spot both of them BEHIND you, having taken advantage of your bizarre piloting choices. You try to pull a maneuver similar to the sneaky method the Black Angel was trying to use before, but no amount of fancy piloting seems to be able to shake your adversary. As you desperately try to make your escape, the Black Angel releases a volley of laser fire at you, blowing you to atoms.

YOU ARE DEAD. CONTINUE: Y/N?
Y: Head to 43 ●●● N: Head to 242 ●●●

• • •

As the saying goes, the west is the best, so you head off toward the Village Gate. This path looks "normal," if that term could be applied to anything happening to you right now—sure, it's an avenue through a graveyard that you've already determined is the home of at least one undead creature, but if you ignore the bones spilling out of the open tombs and littering the ground, you could almost be in a quaint old cemetery back home. Almost.

Soon you come to the Village Gate. The way through is barred, naturally, the two gates that form the barrier held together in the middle by a lock that looks as if it was made from bone and carved to look like a leering skull. Spooky.

Looking down, you realize that beneath your feet and directly in front of the gate is a gigantic, flat grave marker made out of marble that has cracked with age. Your curiosity ignited, you kneel down to investigate. Dirt and debris obscure the name of whoever is buried beneath you. *Who could be entombed in such a strange grave?* you wonder.

If you decide to go back to the crossroads of the graveyard, head to 162 ●

If your curiosity gets the better of you, head to 206 ●●●

The Death-King fires another deadly bolt of energy toward you, and you dodge to the left, barely avoiding being burned by the necromantic projectile. Choose again!

Turn back to 138 ●●●●

●

Hoping to avoid the path of destruction, you move to the side of the gate, but unfortunately the ground there isn't stable anymore. It breaks apart and you fall away into nothingness and it's the end.

Head to 242 ●●●

●●

Gritting your teeth, you shoot your lasers at the Black Angel . . . and the ship explodes in a shower of intergalactic fireworks! Not only have you engaged the Galactic Authority's deadliest pilot, but you've triumphed!

Head to 123 ●

●●●

You leap upward, hoping that you can rise above the situation, but the Death-King sweeps its arms up, catching you in midair and causing you to not-so-spontaneously combust.

Head to 242 ●●●

●●●●

Trusting that the Stone-King can't react in time, you move to the right. But it's swifter than it appears, and it brings its hand down and smashes you like a heroic bug. The thought *Maybe I should have jumped* . . . passes through your mind.

YOU ARE DEAD. CONTINUE: Y/N?
Y: Head to 196 ●● N: Head to 242 ●●●

●

You press your special weapon button, hoping for a miracle, but instead you get the voice of your computer saying that your fighter mode is unavailable at this time. Well, you tried, but choose another option before the hover tank attacks!

Head back to 141 ●●●●

●●

Hoping to buy a few moments, you take your craft into a bank hard to the right. But it's no use, for as soon as you do, the Black Angel does the same thing, copying your move exactly. You try to evade the ace's pursuit, but it's no use—you're directly in the sights of the enemy, and before you can figure out another tactic, blaster fire from the Black Angel's laser cannons rips through your craft and reduces it to little bits of space trash.

YOU ARE DEAD. CONTINUE: Y/N?
Y: Head to 43 ●●● **N: Head to 242** ●●●

●●●

Returning to the plaza at the entrance to the village, you notice that nothing has changed. The gate on the right of the plaza is still closed, as is the gate back to the graveyard. The only way out is back up the lane you just came from, so you must have a task to complete there.

"Hey," says the voice from the well. "Hey. Guess what?"

You look down into the well, hoping to catch a glimpse of whatever down there is speaking, but you can't see anything.

"What?" you ask.

"Goblin butt!" A burst of childish snickering echoes up the well.

Shaking your head and sighing, you turn away from the well and go back to the open gate.

"Wait, wait! I've got a million of 'em . . ."

Not wanting to hear any more humor from the well, you speed up and trot back through the gate on the left.

Head to 115 ●

●●●●

You jerk the controls to the right, and the pilot ahead of you takes advantage of your lack of nerve, moving sharply in the other direction and out of range of your lasers. You attempt to correct your course, but it's too late. Two Galactic Authority fighters close ranks behind you and let you have both barrels of their laser guns . . .

YOU ARE DEAD. CONTINUE: Y/N?
Y: Head to 129 ● N: Head to 242 ●●●

●

Sorry, but you are unarmed. Instead of swinging your sword, you cut the air with a few furious chops of your hands, performing a new and very goofy martial art that you made up on the spot. Seeing your awkward motions, the Death-King laughs coldly. "You amuse me, hopeless one," it says. "I won't destroy you . . . yet!" Thanks to the Death-King's arrogance, you've been given another chance, so don't waste it. Choose again!

Head back to 153 ●

●●

You try to move westward, but a tangle of weeds and vines impedes your passage, halting you in your tracks. You don't know why, but you feel as if there is something else you must do before you start the Crypt Quest. Choose again.

Head back to 167 ●

●●●

Hoping to catch the enemy fighter unawares and maybe get a lucky hit, you squeeze off a few laser rounds, but they shoot harmlessly into space.

"Pilot first, fire later, Cadet!" says Sgt. Brixto over the comms link. You're being watched, so don't let the sarge down!

Head back 69 ●

●●●●

Jumping is good. Jumping is fine. You might as well jump. But you should also keep trying to find your way out of here.

Head back to 162 ●

●

Moving forward, you manage to push the Gorillosaur off your mech, causing it to tumble backward. It recovers quickly, though, and gets back to its feet. But this time, it seems more cautious. You are prey to be reckoned with.

Head to 194 ●●

● ●

Feeling bold and a little bit counterintuitive, you decide that the most dangerous way is the BEST way, and you steer C.O.B. toward the right and the deadly corridor of spinning blades!

"What are you doing?!" Sgt. Brixto exclaims, grabbing you by the shoulders. "That's insane! Go the other way!"

But the sergeant's protests quickly turn to amazed silence as C.O.B. executes a series of robot gymnastics, flipping, cartwheeling, and otherwise deftly avoiding every sharp obstacle in his path, until he finally reaches the end of the hall. Some of the Spider-Bots behind him, however, aren't so lucky, and they're chopped to pieces by the blades. But not all of them are destroyed—many of the bots manage to make it through and press on! C.O.B. continues his run. You're almost there!

Head to 153 ● ●

● ● ●

You swing at the toys with your sword, hacking the little jerks to pieces. But whoever the previous proprietor of this store was sure was prolific, for wave after wave after wave of playthings start to attack you. You can't keep up, and even though you are covered by the splinters and sawdust of destroyed toys, there seems to be no end to them, and before long you are overwhelmed, overtired, and . . .

YOU ARE DEAD. CONTINUE: Y/N?
Y: Head to 188 ● **N:** Head to 242 ●●●

●●●●

Pulling back on your control yoke, your space fighter speeds upward, away from the object of your pursuit. "What are you doing, Cadet? You had 'em!" screams Sgt. Brixto over the comms link. And it's the last thing you ever hear, for you've pulled up directly into the path of a group of Galactic Authority fighters, all of whom fire at you at once . . .

YOU ARE DEAD. CONTINUE: Y/N?
Y: Head to 129 ● **N:** Head to 242 ●●●

The Stone-King rears back, preparing to deliver a massive blow and pulverize you into adventuring jelly. What's your plan?

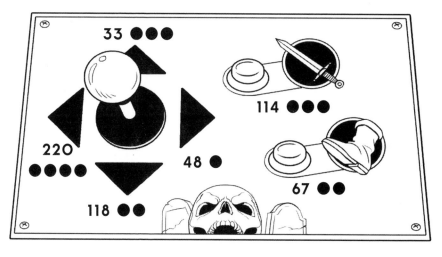

You try to move, but the Gorillosaur anticipates your motion and swiftly jumps on you, this time using its agility to flip over you and grab you from behind. You frantically try to shake the beast off, but it's holding on tight, its jaws snapping at the head of the Walker. Then it climbs up to your Walker's shoulders, grabs its head (which houses your cockpit, of course), and RIPS IT OFF and throws it aside. You watch helplessly as you hurtle through the air. The Gorillosaur stands over the fallen body of the Walker mech, beating its chest victoriously. Then, its celebration finished, it turns toward you and walks over. Kneeling down, it peers into the cockpit, sniffing at it with curiosity. Then once again it howls, and that's when you know that . . .

YOU ARE DEAD. CONTINUE: Y/N?
Y: Head to 68 ●●●● N: Head to 242 ●●●

●●●

You look out your cockpit and see that your pursuit of the Galactic Authority fighter has taken you far away from the action. In the distance, you can see the rapid exchange of laser and missile fire lighting up the darkness of space, highlighted by the occasional explosion. Pulling on your control yoke, you aim your fighter back toward the fray.

"'Scuse me, Sgt. Brixto," you say into your comms link, "but it looks like it's going to take me a little bit of time to get back into it, so while I'm flying, I was hoping you could answer a question for me?"

"Sure thing, Cadet. Ask away."

You pause for a moment, trying to find the right words for what you want to ask.

"What in the name of Neptune is going on?!"

Sgt. Brixto's strange, barking laughter fills your ears. Apparently, he hasn't heard something this funny in quite a while. It takes a few moments for it to subside, and when it does, Sgt. Brixto takes a deep breath and begins to speak.

"You cadets always crack me up, wanting to know 'why' and 'how' and 'what' and all that nonsense. Nobody wants to just fight a Space Battle anymore. No, you all need an epic backstory to motivate ya. Well, I'll give you the short version, since in about a minute or two you're gonna be scrapping again. Check out your comms screen. We worked out a little introductory thing to get new cadets motivated. Coming atcha in three . . . two . . . one . . . now!"

Following Sgt. Brixto's instructions, you watch your comms screen, which has now gone completely dark. There are no maps, readouts, or anything displayed there. Then, these words appear:

SPACE BATTLES!

And as the title becomes clear, music fills your cockpit, a rousing orchestral theme that immediately makes you feel, well, pretty awesome. The two words of the title fade away and are replaced by a readout that unfolds as if it's being typed directly into your computer. It reads:

EVERYTHING HAS GONE SOUTH IN THE
SOLAR SYSTEM. THE GALACTIC AUTHORITY
IS SPREADING ITS AUTHORITARIAN
RULE FROM PLANET TO PLANET, WHICH
IS TOTALLY UNCOOL. AS ITS INFLUENCE
GROWS, CITIZENS OF THE STARS LIVE IN
HOPE THAT SOMEONE, SOMEWHERE CAN
STAND UP TO IT AND BRING BACK FREEDOM.

LUCKILY, A GROUP OF PLUCKY SPACE
PIRATES HAVE RISEN TO THE CHALLENGE.
NORMALLY, THIS GROUP OF NE'ER-DO-WELLS
WOULD BE OUT RAIDING CARGO SHIPS AND
GENERALLY SPREADING THEIR PATENTED
BRAND OF CHAOS ACROSS THE SPACEWAYS,
BUT THE INJUSTICES OF THE GALACTIC
AUTHORITY HAVE BEEN TOO MUCH TO
BEAR, AND SO THEY FIGHT A GUERILLA WAR
AGAINST A FOE THAT OUTNUMBERS AND
OUTGUNS THEM. (THEY'RE BRAVER THAN
THEY ARE SMART.)

WITH A FRESH BATCH OF CADETS AT THE
CONTROLS OF A SQUADRON OF SPACE
FIGHTERS, THE SPACE PIRATES HAVE
COME TO A REMOTE STAR SYSTEM IN THE
HOPES OF UNCOVERING THE GALACTIC
AUTHORITY'S LATEST PLOT WHILE
STRIKING A DECISIVE BLOW AGAINST IT IN
THE PROCESS. BUT LITTLE DO THE SPACE
PIRATES KNOW THAT ON THE PLANET
BELOW, THE GALACTIC AUTHORITY IS
HATCHING A SCHEME THAT MIGHT SPELL
DOOM FOR THEIR RAGTAG REBELLION . . .

As the last word appears on your screen, the music
in the cockpit fades, and you hear Sgt. Brixto curse
over the comms link—or at least, it sounds like he says
something rude, because he's speaking in what sounds
like no language you've ever heard.

"Oh, pardon my Gartraxian, Cadet, but, uh, while
you were reading that introduction some, uh, new
developments have occurred. Take a look behind you."

Head to 43 ●●●

●●●●

Seriously? You've got the Black Angel in your crosshairs and you blow it breaking off in another direction? Have you ever heard the phrase "Snatching defeat from the jaws of victory"? Well, you have now! You probably deserve what happens next, which is piloting your ship directly into a hail of enemy fire. Alas!

YOU ARE DEAD. CONTINUE: Y/N?
Y: Head to 43 ●●● N: Head to 242 ●●●

●

You charge toward the Stone-King . . . and collide with its immovable bulk! Stunned, you're unsteady on your feet for a moment . . . until the giant gently pushes you with one of its fingers and sends you falling down, down, down, into the Almost-Bottomless Well. As you hit the water below, you hear a voice say, "Next time, share your soda."

YOU ARE DEAD. CONTINUE: Y/N?
Y: Head to 196 ●● N: Head to 242 ●●●

"Come on," says Sgt. Brixto as he leads you in the opposite direction of the mad rush to the hangar. "Let them handle the dogfight. You're needed for another mission. This way."

As the base shakes and rocks from what seems to be multiple impacts from heavy explosives, the sergeant leads you deeper and deeper into a maze of corridors until you finally reach your destination: a nondescript door?

"What's up, Sarge?" you ask, but Sgt. Brixto ignores you and inputs a complicated number into the keypad next to the door, which *whooshes* open when he finishes.

"In here. Hurry. We don't have much time."

As you enter the room, you notice that you're in what appears to be some sort of torpedo bay, but the only things in here are a small, comfortable-looking chair with a control yoke and a screen in front of it, a torpedo tube, and a spindly three-foot-tall humanoid robot, standing at strict attention.

"This little guy is the Space Pirates' latest weapon in the fight against the Galactic Authority, and you two together are going to help us take down Slaystation Omega. Lieutenant, meet your next piloting job: the

Covert Operations Bot, or C.O.B., for short."

You have to admit, C.O.B.'s kind of cute, especially after he silently and properly salutes you and then stands back at attention. Amazed, you return the salute.

"C.O.B. here might look like a little twerp, but he's actually a sophisticated stealth bot, meant to infiltrate tough-to-reach spots," Sgt. Brixto continues. "And that's where YOU come in. Get in the launch tube, C.O.B."

At Sgt. Brixto's command, the small robot nimbly climbs into the torpedo launch tube.

"Here's the drill: We have no hope of defeating Slaystation Omega with our starships. They can only distract it. We have to destroy it from the inside, and that's where you and C.O.B. come in. Y'see, we're gonna shoot C.O.B. out of this torpedo bay AT that crazy thing, and YOU'RE going to pilot him there remotely. If he gets inside, you're going to guide him through the Slaystation and to its control center, where you'll detonate him. Oh yeah, did I mention that C.O.B.'s also a bomb? Well, he is. Aren't you, C.O.B.?"

At that, C.O.B. snaps off another salute and lies down, the tube sealing itself over his body.

"Ah, that little guy's cute. Too bad you've gotta blow him up. So: You ready for this?"

You sit down at the control console. This is it. Beat this and you beat *Space Battles*. You turn to Sgt. Brixto and mimic C.O.B.'s snappy salute. The crusty old salt smiles a toothy, terrifying grin.

"Let's do this, Cadet. I mean, Corporal. Um, excuse me, LIEUTENANT. Launching C.O.B.!"

Sgt. Brixto presses a button, and *BOOM*—C.O.B. is shot into space toward Slaystation Omega. On the screen you see the little robot's progress through his eyes: he zooms through the battle raging out in space, bypassing the laser fire all around, getting closer and closer and closer and closer to his gigantic target until . . . *BANG!* He collides with the hull of the fearsome Slaystation, sticking to its surface thanks to his built-in magnets. You watch your screen with fascination as C.O.B. swiftly crawls to find an access port, weaseling his way in, then sneaking through ducts and passageways until, finally, he's standing in an interior corridor.

"All right, here's the deal," Sgt. Brixto says. "C.O.B.'s got a tracker inside him that will make him move forward toward the core of the Slaystation constantly, so all you have to worry about is making the correct move left or right at any intersection you come to. Once you get C.O.B. into the control center . . . detonate him."

On the screen, C.O.B. gives a solemn thumbs-up.

"We've got the element of surprise on our side, so all you need to do is get him there. Use those amazing instincts of yours and get 'er done."

On the screen, you can see that something has gotten C.O.B.'s attention—he's been stealthily surrounded by a group of mechanical arachnids, which circle him like they're hunters about to move in for the kill.

"Blast! They've got Spider-Bots! They're security robots. The enemy must have detected an intruder and sent 'em to clean it out! Those things are nasty, sneaky, and fast. If they get C.O.B. before he gets to the control center, this operation is OVER. Okay, Lieutenant," says Sgt. Brixto. "It's time to blow some stuff up. Go, C.O.B., go!"

And C.O.B., chased by skittering Spider-Bots, moves into the mazelike interior of Slaystation Omega.

Leaping over junk and squeezing through narrow gaps, he barely keeps a few steps ahead of the robotic death-arachnids in pursuit. Ahead of you, you can see the fork in the corridor you're in: On the right, it looks as if it narrows into a tunnel that C.O.B. will have to crawl through. On the left, darkness. Which way do you go?

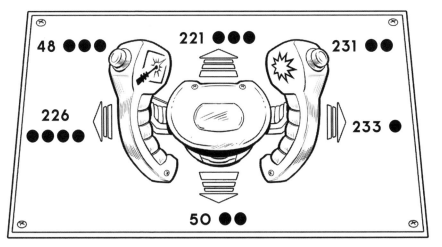

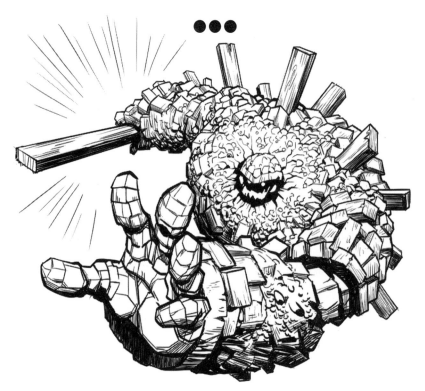

The Stone-King has you weaponless and cornered, but you've still got some life. What's your play?

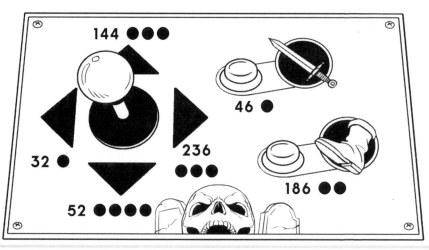

●●●●

As the Gorillosaur rushes forward, you move the Walker to the side, hoping to avoid its charge and buy yourself some time. But as you do, the monster grabs the Walker by its arm and pulls . . . tearing a robotic limb from your robotic body! Screaming in triumph, the Gorillosaur raises your former arm like a club and proceeds to beat your mech with it over and over and over. You raise your mech's other arm, hoping to hold off the assault, but it's no use. The Gorillosaur, enraged, reduces your mech (and you) into a pile of scrap metal. Perhaps in the future, new generations of Gorillosaurs will worship this pile of scrap metal as some sort of sacred object. Hey, it could happen.

YOU ARE DEAD. CONTINUE: Y/N?
Y: Head to 68 ●●●● N: Head to 242 ●●●

●

Eagerly trying to keep up with the Galactic Authority fighter, you pull your yoke to the left. Unfortunately, the fighter you're pursuing edges to the right, and you lose them! Try again.

Head back to 69 ●

●●

With more bravery than common sense, you plunge headlong toward the Death-King's fireball . . . and are shocked to discover that the projectile was actually an ILLUSION! How about that? The Death-King is a big faker!

Continue to 62 ●●●

●●●

C'mon. Cut it out. This is a joke, right? Trying to use the special weapon again? Okay, we'll give you a pass on this one because you've got moxie. Choose again.

Head back to 218 ●●●●

●●●●

If there was no going back before (thanks to C.O.B.'s programming), there's DEFINITELY no going back now (because of both programming and the fact that you've almost reached your goal). Keep going and pick another move!

Head back to 153 ●●

You press the special weapon button, fully expecting it to be a bust like before, but . . . no! What's this? Something NEW is happening. Something WEIRD. This time, instead of setting off an annoying buzzer, the special weapon seems to have started a process within your ship. You can feel its parts rearranging, gears moving, everything shifting. The cockpit starts to rise, and in moments, you can see that your space fighter has become something decidedly different.

"Congratulations," you hear the ship's computer voice say. "You have unlocked . . . WALKER MODE!"

Head to 166

●●●●

●●

You've scrambled forward, through the Skele-King's legs, and now you stand BEHIND the undead giant, and although your bold move has confused it for a moment, it's now turning to find you. What do you do?

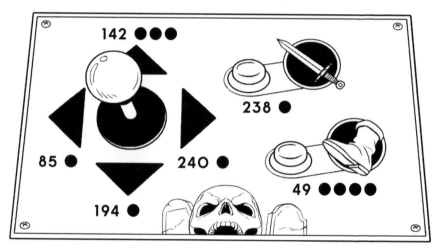

●●●

You know that you can't give up, so you figure that maybe if you attack again and again and again, perhaps you can wear the Stone-King down. Once more your sword has no effect, only this time, things get about a thousand times worse as the Stone-King knocks your sword aside and out of your hand! You are now unarmed. But still, you live.

Head to 110 ●●●

●●●●

You jam your control yoke to the left, and as your targeting guide passes over the Black Angel . . . the ship disappears completely. You went after the wrong one! You pull back to the right, hoping to correct your mistake, but the Black Angel is a step ahead of you and has already turned around to come at you head-on, guns a-blazing! Surprised and shocked, you try to pull up and avoid the Black Angel's lasers, but it's no use. You're caught, and . . .

YOU ARE DEAD. CONTINUE: Y/N?
Y: Head to 43 ●●● **N:** Head to 242 ●●●

●

With caution bred by your recent experiences in the graveyard and knowing that you don't really have any choice, you start to skulk down the street on the left, away from the plaza. You find yourself in a cramped lane paved by cobblestones. On either side of you are buildings that look to be dwellings and businesses that haven't been occupied in hundreds of years, years that have been unkind, as the buildings themselves sag and lean against one another, each preventing its neighbor from falling over. You're afraid that if you tried to open one of the closed doors, you might set off a chain reaction of destruction, the buildings falling like dominoes and burying you alive.

Soon, after some twists and turns, you come to a dead end, a cul-de-sac bordered by three buildings. The building on your left has a sign above it that reads "Ye Olde Provisions Shoppe." The building directly ahead has a sign hanging over the door that reads "Ye Olde Toy Shoppe." And the building to your right has the words "Ye Olde Certain Doom Shoppe" carved into the wood of its doorframe. Unlike every other building you've passed so far, the doors on these buildings are OPEN.

You're at a dead end. Where would you like to go?

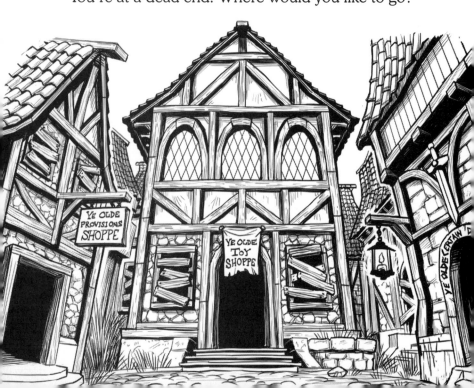

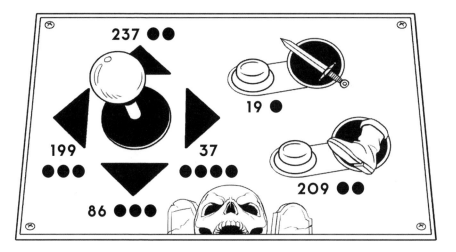

Nope. Try again.

Head back to 194 ●●

●●●

You move to the right, barely avoiding the orb of fiery death that rockets down the hall, but strangely, there's no heat coming from it—it was an illusion! But it seems as if this was all part of the Death-King's plan. It was a distraction, and the Death-King is no longer there! The corridor it stood in is now closed, and the fire from the ballroom has caught up to you!

Head to 242 ●●●

●●●●

You try to fire your lasers, but you can't get a bead on an opponent this close, and your shots fly wild into the sky. Choose another option!

Head back to 218 ●●●●

●

You push your ship into a dive, barrel-rolling while you're at it, and this tricky maneuver allows you to evade the Galactic Authority ship headed at you AND the hot death of its lasers. Correcting your course, you pull around . . . and discover that the same fighter is once again headed straight at you!

"Try it again, Cadet!" snaps Sgt. Brixto over your comms link.

Head back to 179 ●

●●

You edge backward just as the Stone-King strikes! You avoid being crushed, but just barely, and you've bought yourself another second to think. Choose another action!

Head back to 99 ●

● ● ●

Wow. The Black Angel is behind you, and you just want to shoot off your lasers? That's just bizarre. Well, that's your right, but it's certainly not going to help. In fact, the Black Angel comes back on your comms link for a moment to gloat evilly.

"This is the best that the Space Pirates can send against me? The Black Angel?! Ha ha ha ha*RBZZZKT*!"

The evil gloating is cut short as the Black Angel unleashes a volley of laser fire at you, with predictable results.

YOU ARE DEAD. CONTINUE: Y/N?
Y: Head to 43 ● ● ● N: Head to 242 ● ● ●

● ● ● ●

C.O.B. has successfully made his way through the strange catwalk-over-a-lava-pit room, and you can tell that the bot is getting agitated, as if he senses something.

"The little guy's programming is telling 'im that he's gettin' close to wherever he needs to be," Sgt. Brixto says. "You're almost there. Don't screw this up."

Looking around, you can see that there are, once again, two ways that C.O.B. can go. To C.O.B.'s left, there's what looks to be a fairly unremarkable corridor, from which you can hear the sounds of activity. Could the command station be that way? Perhaps. To the right, however, is another strange example of Galactic Authority Slaystation layout: It's a hallway, but a wild assortment of blades and other sharp implements of death spin at seemingly random, but rapid, intervals. It's a whirling hall of knives! So: Which way looks promising to you? Think quick—the Spider-Bots are still behind C.O.B.!

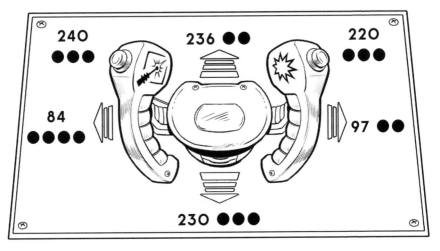

You try to move, but the Gorillosaur anticipates your motion and swiftly jumps on you, this time using its agility to flip over you and grab you from behind. You frantically try to shake the beast off, but it's holding on tight, its jaws snapping at the head of the Walker. Then it climbs up to your Walker's shoulders, grabs its head (which houses your cockpit, of course), and RIPS IT OFF and throws it aside. You watch helplessly as you hurtle through the air. The Gorillosaur stands over the fallen body of the Walker mech, beating its chest victoriously. Then, its celebration finished, it turns toward you and walks over. Kneeling down, it peers into the cockpit, sniffing at it with curiosity. Then once again it howls, and that's when you know that . . .

YOU ARE DEAD. CONTINUE: Y/N?
Y: Head to 68 ●●●● N: Head to 242 ●●●

●●

You rush toward the right to pursue the Death-King but pass through its body—it's another illusion! You chose poorly! And when you try to retrace your steps, you find that a magical barrier has sealed the doorway. You pound on it with your fists to no avail—you are trapped! And that's when you hear the strange growling noises coming from the darkness behind you: Someone—or someTHING—is trapped in this corridor with you, and it's coming closer . . . closer . . . closer. You can see its bloodshot eyes almost glowing in the darkness, but that's not the worst part. No, the worst part is when it opens its mouth and you can see its teeth. Hundreds of shiny, razor-sharp teeth . . .

Head to 242 ●●●

●●●

Moving in this direction was your first—and last—mistake, for you've piloted your Walker into a newly formed chasm in the floor of the jungle. As you plummet, your Walker collides with and scrapes against the sides of the hole you're falling down, and you try to grasp hold of anything that will arrest your momentum, but nothing works. There's no doubt about it . . .

YOU ARE DEAD. CONTINUE: Y/N?
Y: Head to 56 ●● N: Head to 242 ●●●

●●●●

You cautiously move toward your seemingly incapacitated opponent, wary that its apparent distress could be a ruse. It's this caution which proves to be your undoing, for as you creep closer, the Death-King moves its hands in a complicated gesture. They begin to glow, and too late do you realize that your foul nemesis has one last trick up its sleeve.

"If I must die, so will YOU," the Death-King says, laughing bitterly. The light from its hands explodes outward, consuming the Death-King, the throne room, and yes, YOU. You hesitated and, sadly, you have LOST.

Head to 242 ●●●

●

"That was some amazing flying, Cadet," says Sgt. Brixto as he appears on your comms screen. He's grinning proudly, an expression that, frankly, looks pretty scary on a mug like his. "A kill like that, well, that sort of victory is the type of thing that gives us Space Pirates the edge over the Galactic Authority. We might win this hopeless struggle yet, with pilots like YOU on our side. In fact, the Space Pirates' high command wants to thank you for your service with a reward. You've been promoted, you lucky so-and-so!"

CONGRATULATIONS! YOU HAVE BEEN PROMOTED TO THE RANK OF SPACE PIRATE CORPORAL!

"How about that?" Sgt. Brixto says, amazed. "In all my years of Space Piracy, I've never seen a rookie get promoted that fast. Incredible. In fact, it reminds me of this one time—"

But Sgt. Brixto's reminiscing is cut short as alarms begin to blare in your cockpit. You look around frantically, trying to figure out what's wrong, when *BOOM!* An explosion erupts behind you, interrupting your brief moment of jubilation. The lasers of a straggling Galactic Authority ship have ignited your engine. Another Space Pirates ship swoops in and dispatches the attacker, but the damage has been done: The controls on your fighter are unresponsive.

"Cadet!" you hear Sgt. Brixto yell as your ship begins to dive toward the nearby planet. "I mean, Corporal! Pull up! Pull*BZZZZZZT!*"

Sgt. Brixto's communication is cut off, and try as you might, your controls are unresponsive, and you descend down, down, down . . .

Down through the planet's atmosphere, which causes your ship to glow with incredible heat . . .

Down through the heavy cloud cover, which obscures the planet's surface and buffets your fighter to and fro . . .

And then, finally, down toward the canopy of what looks to be a huge, mountainous JUNGLE. Your controls are still unresponsive, but through the static on your comms unit, you begin to hear the voice of Sgt. Brixto once again.

". . . you hear me? Corporal, can you hear me? Come in, Corporal."

You mutter a reply and can hear the sergeant exhale with relief.

"Phew! Thought I lost you there for a second. I've got good news and bad news for you. Bad news first: You're about to crash into the jungle."

"What's the good news, Sergeant?" you ask.

"If you survive the crash, your ship's auto-repair systems should be able to get it functional enough so it can transform into Tank Walker mode. That's a big if, though."

"What's Tank Walker mode?"

"You'll see soon enough. Or maybe not. Hang on. See you on the other side. Impact in ten . . . nine . . . eight . . ."

You notice that the distance between your ship and the top of the jungle has lessened considerably. *Gulp*.

"Seven . . . six . . . five . . ."

It's even less now. You think you can see weird alien birds in the trees. You hold your breath reflexively.

"Four . . . three . . . two . . . one . . . Impact!"

As your ship tears into the tops of the trees, the cockpit fills with what can only be described as an Intergalactic Airbag, which braces your body while you crash through foliage and are shaken so hard you pass out.

Head to 56 ●●

●●

You hope to outflank your enemy by banking to the left, but with your attention focused on the Black Angel, you don't have enough time to react to another Galactic Authority fighter swooping in, headed directly at you, lasers blazing. You try to squeeze off a shot, but it's too late.

YOU ARE DEAD. CONTINUE: Y/N?
Y: Head to 43 ●●● N: Head to 242 ●●●

●●●

Moving to the right, you watch the Death-King suspiciously. What if this is some sort of ruse, with the intent of catching you off guard? As you step carefully, the Death-King turns and, from its raised hand, shoots a blast of awful energy in your direction. Thankfully, you saw the attack coming, and you deftly move to the side, allowing the killing blow to pass by and blow a hole in the wall behind you. That was close, but close only counts in horseshoes and hand grenades, not death magic. Give it another go!

Head back to 20 ●●

●●●●

Your punch lands, and you're surprised that you didn't break your hand on the Stone-King's rough exterior. In fact, your fist tears through the monster's "flesh," and a chain reaction begins. The Flame Key ignites and, impossibly, its fire spreads to the Stone-King, rapidly traveling up its body and causing it to slap at its arms and legs in the hope of extinguishing the enchanted blaze. But it's no use, and the Stone-King begins to quickly break apart, its bricks and mortar and ash spilling into the Almost-Bottomless Well, sealing it.

"Mmph, mmph!" comes a cry from below: the voice, probably trying to beg you to remove some of the debris. Ignoring the faint whining, you pick up your sword. You have claimed the Flame Key and defeated the Stone-King. Your next mission? Move on to the next challenge, the one that will bring you closer to beating *Crypt Quest*. New treasure in hand, you leave the plaza (ignoring more muffled protests from the now-sealed Almost-Bottomless Well) and exit the Abandoned Village through the now-open gate. Making haste, you jog through the graveyard, make a left at the crossroads, and head into the freezing corridor that heralds your approach to the next gate. Before long, you're standing in a chilly mess of ice and bones. You've reached your destination. You've reached . . .

Head to 28 ●●●

The *Space Battles* machine, with its cabinet illustrations depicting a ridiculous dogfight among starships, mecha-esque robots, and cool hover tanks, calls out to you—you feel the need to become a roguish pilot in the middle of an intergalactic conflict, and the sounds of dramatic music, laser cannons, and fiery explosions that blast from the machine only make that desire stronger. Placing a hand on the futuristic-looking yoke below the screen, you drop your token into the coin slot and press the Start button.

BOOM! The Midnight Arcade begins to rumble as if it's being shaken by the power of a star-drive warming up for a launch. The lights on everything around you go out in an instant. Only the *Space Battles* machine stays lit, and you hold on as if your life depends on it. The rumbling gets louder, and a bright light begins to shine on you from above. But this is no ordinary light. You can feel it taking your body apart, turning you into pure energy until you disappear entirely—you are being transported! But to where?

Almost as soon as you disappear, you reappear, but you're no longer in the Midnight Arcade. Looking around in wonder, you see that you're in a massive hangar full of small space fighters just like the ones on the side of the *Space Battles* machine—in fact, you're standing next to one!

Looking down at yourself, you see that you're dressed in a sleek flight suit and carrying a helmet. Adding to the confusion, deafening alert horns are blaring all around you, and beings of all shapes, colors, and sizes are running around the hangar in a mad state of emergency. They all look to be preparing their ships for launch, and at the end of the hangar, ships are taking off into what looks like outer space, and, if the laser blasts and explosions are any indication, joining what looks like an actual SPACE BATTLE.

Whoa.

As you take in the chaos around you, through the crowd you catch the eyes (well, eye—there's an eye patch where one of its eyes would be) of a short, green-furred humanoid dressed in a flight suit similar to yours. It kind of looks like a chimpanzee crossed with an orc, and noticing you, it scowls and walks your way. "Cadet!" the alien barks. "First off, even though we're Space Pirates, you salute your superior when you see him."

It's only now that you notice the name tag on the creature's left chest that reads SGT. BRIXTO. You snap out an awkward salute, still wondering: *How did I get here? What's going ON?* But the creature—sorry, Sgt. Brixto—interrupts your reverie.

"Second: Are you gonna stand there all day and gawk, or are you going to get in your ship?"

You continue to stand and gawk at the tumult around you, and the creature laughs.

"Yeah, I was just like you when I was a green recruit. I don't think I closed my mouth for a week when I joined up! But this isn't the time for sightseeing—it's time for action!"

Brixto jerks his thumb at the ladder leading to the ship's cockpit.

"Now, what are you waiting for? Put on that helmet and get in that ship before I kick you out of the air lock!"

Nodding, you obey the sergeant's order, jamming the helmet on your head and climbing up the ladder to the cockpit of the space fighter. Settling into its snug seat, you see that you're surrounded by a variety of knobs, switches, panels, readouts, and other things that you have no idea what they are. As you look around in confusion, you feel the engine of your space fighter begin to hum—it's on! The canopy shield closes, sealing you in, and your ship starts to slowly lift off from the hangar floor! Once again, you feel panic rise within you.

Frantically, you start to slap at the control panels around you, pushing buttons and flipping switches randomly. Immediately you realize that you've made a mistake, for your ship starts to spin around wildly, causing the beings in the hangar to run and duck in panic. As you try to figure out what you've done wrong, the familiar face of Sgt. Brixto appears on one of the screens in front of you, and he doesn't look happy.

"What in the name of Praxis IV are you doing, Cadet? Get that ship under control NOW before you kill us all.

That's an order! First things first: Take a deep breath and grab that control yoke in front of you. Look familiar?"

You look at the controls of the space fighter and realize that, yes, they remind you of something you saw recently, something very familiar . . . That's it! Before you is the exact same controller that was on the *Space Battles* machine back in the Midnight Arcade! It looks like this:

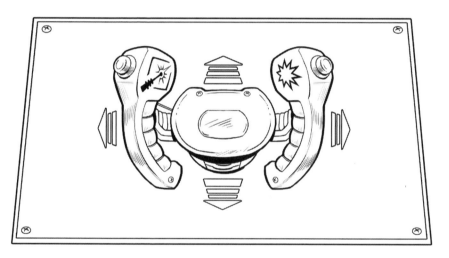

"That's your control yoke, y'see? Push forward on it to dive, pull back to climb. Move left and right to, well, move left and right. The button on the left stick is for your laser guns, the button on the right is only for emergencies. Got it?"

Realizing that panicking won't help anything, you relax as your now-floating ship begins moving forward, out of the air lock and toward the Space Battle. "Got it," you reply.

"Good! We'll handle the thrust, so you just pilot this thing and try not to get vaporized by those Galactic Authority Fighters out there. Activating thrust . . . now!"

You're pushed back into your chair for a moment as your space fighter accelerates out of the hangar and toward the battle.

In a moment, one of the screens in front of you blurs with static and then resolves into an image of Sgt. Brixto, who looks amused at your obvious distress.

"What's going on, Sergeant?" you ask, your voice cracking with nervousness. Sgt. Brixto laughs.

"Ha! What a greenie. I take back what I said—I've NEVER seen any cadet like you before. What's going on? An epic battle between good and evil is what's going on. Us Space Pirates versus the Galactic Authority. But as long as you listen to me, you'll be okay—at least until you get vaporized, that is! Ha ha ha! That's a joke, Cadet.

"No time like the present to get your ears wet," he barks. "You know what we say in the Space Pirates: Let's go get 'em!"

The image of Sgt. Brixto on your display glitches out for a moment and is replaced by a digital readout of these words:

Looking around, you see that you're in a phalanx of similar space fighters, sleek and deadly-looking, and that you're all headed for the same destination: a cluster of bug-like enemy fighters that are screaming toward YOU. Grasping the control yoke as they get closer, you know that it's time to be a PILOT. So what do you do?

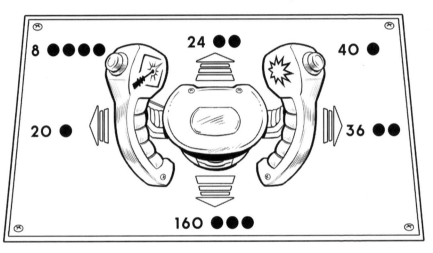

The Hortiskull writhes and wiggles before you, screeching an unearthly keen while menacing you with its awful, vine-like arms and terrible chomping jaws. It looks like it's come from the deepest, darkest part of the swamp, this awful thing, and it smells like a pile of lawn clippings that have been sitting forgotten in a trash can for weeks in the middle of summer. While watching its tendrils move, you realize that the way it's rhythmically performing the same limited action over and over is kind of like an idle animation in a video game. Weird.

What's your move?

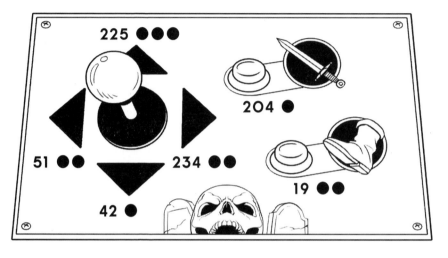

Sword in hand, you jog west along the graveyard's wall, figuring that if you follow it, you'll eventually reach the gate that leads to the sad-looking village you saw when you were on top of the tomb. *Maybe I'll find someone there to help me*, you think. But you quickly dismiss that thought once you remember that you're in a haunted video game and you're probably headed toward some new sort of peril or enemy.

Before too long, you come to a corner of the

graveyard. Ahead, the rubble-strewn path continues toward the western gate. So far, so good, but are you absolutely sure you want to go this way?

If you want to keep heading toward the Village Gate, head to 90 ●●●

If you want to head back toward where you began, head to 76 ●●●

●●●●

"It seems as though I have underestimated you," the Death-King says with a sneer in its voice. "No longer. Now, prepare to be CRUSHED! DESTROYED! ANNIHILATED UTTERLY! Bwa ha ha ha ha!" Are you going to let it talk to you like that? Make a move!

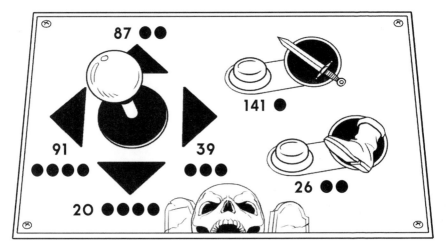

87 ●●

141 ●

91 ●●●●

39 ●●●

26 ●●

20 ●●●●

●

Noting that the path to the left seems to be clear, you pilot your Walker in that direction. And not a moment too soon, for as you move, the earth beneath where you were just standing crumbles into nothingness, leaving behind a hole that looks, for all intents and purposes, bottomless. Heedless of your direction, you keep moving until you feel the tremors subside. Pausing for a moment, you turn back and see a completely altered landscape. What IS it with this planet and sudden death lurking around every corner, anyway?

Head to 176 ● ● ● ●

● ●

Nope, that still doesn't work. Luckily, figuring that out takes less than a second, so you have the opportunity to try something else. Don't waste this second chance!

Head back to 43 ● ● ●

● ● ●

In a fit of inspiration, you decide that here goes nothing, and you drive your sword directly down into the Skele-King's skull. As it turns out, that's its weak spot, and you cleave it in two and cause its body to go limp, then fall apart. Victory! The Skele-King's body crumbles, now utterly lifeless, and you land safely on the ground as it falls. What remains is now a ruined mess of regular bone and dusty clothes, but while you were battling the creature, you noticed something, and you begin to dig through its remains. Tossing ulnas, metacarpals, scapulas, and other bones you can't name aside, you eventually find what you are looking for . . .

CONGRATULATIONS! YOU HAVE ACQUIRED

THE SKELETON KEY!

It's time to ramble on. Where do you want to go?

If you want to explore the rest of the graveyard, go to the crossroads by turning to 162 ●

If you want to use the Skeleton Key, head to 188 ●

●●●●

The Galactic Authority troops have retreated, but you're still facing off against one of the enemy's hover tanks, and your lasers seemingly have no effect on its thick armor. A fallen tree trunk is directly behind you, and the tank looks like it's about to fire another blast at you, maybe the blast that'll finish you off. What do you do?

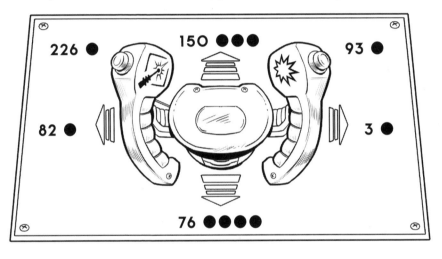

●

The Death-King unleashes another bolt of deadly energy in your direction, and the only thing you can think of doing is raising your sword in the hopes of somehow deflecting the blow. It takes all of your strength to hold on to your blade, but you do. And something surprising has happened—somehow, you've deflected the killing beam BACK at the Death-King! It strikes the cloaked figure, causing it to crumple to the ground in a smoking heap, injured but not quite defeated.

Head to 20 ●●

●●

Thrusters firing, you force your fighter to dive, and instantly you lose sight of your enemy. Why did you do that? You'll never know, but you do know this: Diving directly into an oncoming squadron of Galactic Authority fighters might not have been the best move at this point.

YOU ARE DEAD. CONTINUE: Y/N?
Y: Head to 43 ●●● **N: Head to 242** ●●●

●●●

What? You just came from there! Well, you run back through the Skele-King's legs, and this time it's ready for you, snatching you with one of its bony claws and tossing you into the air. As you fly over the tombstones, you realize that, barring a miracle . . .

YOU ARE DEAD. CONTINUE: Y/N?
Y: Head to 167 ● **N: Head to 242** ●●●

●●●●

As the Gorillosaur rushes forward, you move the Walker to the side, hoping to avoid its charge and buy yourself some time. But as you do, the monster grabs the Walker by its arm and pulls . . . tearing a robotic limb from your robotic body! Screaming in triumph, the Gorillosaur raises your former arm like a club and proceeds to beat your mech with it over and over and over. You raise your mech's other arm, hoping to hold off the assault, but it's no use. The Gorillosaur, enraged, reduces your mech (and you) into a pile of scrap metal. Perhaps in the future, new generations of Gorillosaurs will worship this pile of scrap metal as some sort of sacred object. Hey, it could happen.

YOU ARE DEAD. CONTINUE: Y/N?
Y: Head to 68 ●●●● **N:** Head to 242 ●●●

●

You retreat from the Death-King's phantasmic projectile, and it looks as if you've avoided the worst, but your opponent jerks its hands upward, and you're enveloped in magical flame. For a moment you run around the throne room, setting fire to cobwebs and moldy drapes, but you are quickly consumed, your wild perambulations halted forever. Alas!

Head to 242 ●●●

●●

You try evasive action in a desperate attempt to avoid the terrible gaze of Slaystation Omega, but it SEES you. You climb, you dive, you bank to the left and to the right, but its gaze follows you, inexorably, ultimately catching up to your ship and breaking it (and you) into a million pieces.

Head to 242 ●●●

●●●

Throwing caution to the wind, you run toward the Stone-King for some strange reason, and you promptly become a pancake underneath its crushing blow.

YOU ARE DEAD. CONTINUE: Y/N?
Y: Head to 196 ●● N: Head to 242 ●●●

●●●●

The Galactic Authority fighter tries to shake you by pulling up, but you pull up as well, keeping them in view. You're still hot on their tail.

Head to 23 ●

Sword in hand, you trot east along the graveyard's wall, assuming that if you go this way, you'll soon come to the gate that looked like it led to the swamp. Maybe it's there that you'll find the answers you're looking for? *It's possible*, you think, *but it's even more likely that what lies ahead is a lot more fighting creatures, dodging obstacles, and assorted other video game "fun."*

Soon (and much to your surprise), you arrive at the corner of the graveyard without meeting any resistance. In front of you is the path that will take you toward the eastern gate. From where you stand, you can see that in a few yards the path is obscured by a light fog that carries a whiff of swamp gas. You can still change your mind and backtrack.

If you want to keep heading toward the Swamp Gate, head to 173 ●

If you want to head back toward where you began, head to 76 ●●●

●●

The Gorillosaur has fallen and, from the looks of it, cannot get up and won't get up ever again. You've faced every obstacle this freaky planet could throw at you, and somehow, you've survived. As if on cue, your comms screen lights up, and once again Sgt. Brixto's face appears there, only this time he doesn't look happy or even surprised. No, if anything, he looks PROUD.

"We watched that battle from up here, Corporal, and let me tell you that what you did . . . well, it was just amazing."

You try to brush off the praise, but he's not hearing it.

"Don't be modest! That was some fantastic mech-vs.-monster fighting, the likes of which I haven't seen since I was scrapping with Gorillosaurs back in the day. Glad I don't have to do THAT anymore. I mean, sure, that was a small one, but whatever size those things are, what a pain in the tuchus, I'm telling you. And hey, it looks like Space Pirates high command was watching, too! They've got another present for you."

Sgt. Brixto's face disappears from your screen and is promptly replaced by this:

CONGRATULATIONS! YOU HAVE BEEN PROMOTED TO THE RANK OF SPACE PIRATE LIEUTENANT!

"Well, don't that beat all," Sgt. Brixto says when he reappears on the screen. "You outrank me! Well, technically. I'm still yer boss as far as I'm concerned, and I order you to strap that mech into that booster rocket and get up here—we need ya!"

You snap off a salute and move your Walker mech forward, positioning the robot with its back to the rocket. As you get closer, magnetic clamps on your back engage with a satisfying CLUNK, securely attaching your mech to the transport.

"All right, you're all hooked up," Sgt. Brixto says. "Sending coordinates to your computer now. See ya soon!"

A string of numbers appears on your screen as the cold voice of your onboard computer begins to speak.

"Destination: confirmed. Space Pirates base. Priming booster rocket."

A low whine sounds from the booster rocket.

"Activating booster rocket."

The low whine turns into a quiet rumble as the engine begins to power up.

"Launch in ten . . . nine . . . eight . . ."

The rumble grows in volume and strength, shaking the mech violently.

". . . seven . . . six . . . five . . ."

The rumbling from the rocket has now reached a seemingly critical stage, to the point that you think that if you don't take off soon, you'll either be shaken to nuts and bolts or explode.

". . . four . . . three . . . two . . . one . . . Liftoff."

A great gout of flame erupts from the booster rocket, and in moments, your Walker mech is aloft, quickly speeding away from the remains of the Space Pirates base, the body of the Gorillosaur, and the planet itself. Soon, the terrific thrust of the rocket mellows, and you no longer feel as if your fillings are about to pop out of your teeth. You relax as you leave the planet's atmosphere, the guidance system in the mech steering you toward some lights in the distance, around which dance smaller lights, like fireflies at night. As you get closer, you see that the bigger lights are actually on the Space Pirates' massive main flagship, and the smaller ones are fighter ships, like the one you piloted, zipping to and fro around the base. Two of the ships break away and zoom over to you, each of them taking up position on either side of your mech. They're an escort! As your vehicle approaches the hangar of the Space Pirates base, you slow down dramatically, and once inside, you hover for a moment as the rocket gently deposits your mech feetfirst upon the deck. The rocket powers down, and your cockpit opens. Climbing up a ladder, you exit the mech, standing on its shoulder and observing the mad dash of activity in the hangar. As you gaze about it in wonder, a small hover platform carrying Sgt. Brixto floats over to you.

"Still gawking like a green cadet, eh? Pfft. Figures. Hop on."

You leap onto the floating platform, and Sgt. Brixto shakes his head.

"Anyway, there's no time to stand around and congratulate yourself for your upward mobility in the ranks—big stuff is happening, and we've got a briefing now. Ready for some more action?"

You nod confidently.

"Good. Because you're about to get it."

Head to 78 ●●●●

●●●

You attempt to move somewhere, anywhere, to avoid the next blast from the hover tank's cannon, but no matter which direction you go, the barrel of its weapon tracks you . . . and then fires! And as it turns out, your Walker can't survive another blast. This one cripples it, causing a complete systems shutdown. The legs on the mech seize up, and the vehicle topples over, with you inside. You black out for a moment, then come to, and when you do, you see Galactic Authority troops surrounding your cockpit, weapons aimed straight at you through the cracked glass. It looks like they're waiting for the command to fire. And then one of them speaks up.

"All right . . . fire!"

And they do. Ouch.

YOU ARE DEAD. CONTINUE: Y/N?
Y: Head to 56 ●● N: Head to 242 ●●●

●●●●

The Abominable Snowmancer points at you, and a ray of ice comes from its outstretched hand. Luckily, you have your wits about you, and you jump up just in time and avoid getting hit by the freezing blast. Turning, you see that the blast is forming a wall of ice that is blocking the path back to the graveyard crossroads. You nimbly hop onto the side of a nearby tomb, and then jump to another outcropping of rock, and then on top of the shoulders of one of those nearby statues, nearly losing your balance and falling in the process. The wall of ice now blocks your way, but with one final leap . . .

. . . you JUST make it over and fall to the ground on the other side, away from the wrath of the Abominable Snowmancer. You can hear its howls of frustration, though, and over the top of the wall come hunks of ice and snow. *I'm not ready yet*, you think. *If this is a game, I've got to learn some stuff before I face the final boss.* And with that, you make haste back to the graveyard's crossroads.

Head back to 162 ●

●

The Stone-King swings its beam-club, and you react quickly enough to clear its path by just barely leaping over it. You land on your two feet, ready for your next action.

Head to 99 ●

●●

You press the button for your laser, and . . . C.O.B. does a nifty cartwheel!

Wait, what?

That's right, he does a cartwheel. And his form is great. But he keeps running into the core of the Slaystation, and it's time for you to choose another move. Go for it.

Head back to 153 ●●

●●●

You draw backward just as the Stone-King brings its melee weapon down in front of you, missing you by inches!

Head to 99 ●

●●●●

Once again, your special weapon turns out to be nothing special, really. Try again.

Head back to 41 ●●●

"You're very lucky," hisses the Death-King as it walks toward you. "But now you have no sword! It seems that your luck has run out!" You realize that the fiend is correct—that last blast sent your weapon flying behind you. What can you possibly do now?!

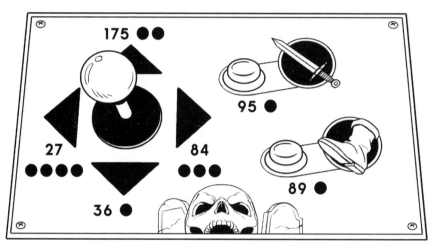

Tailed by the remaining Spider-Bots, C.O.B. emerges into a room full of Galactic Authority scientists and soldiers gathered around control consoles, all centered around what looks to be a gigantic battery of some sort, a power source that has the face of the Slaystation! This is it, the core, the command center, the evil cream-filled center of the diabolical cupcake that is the Galactic Authority.

C.O.B. runs toward the battery face, and as he does, it rotates to look directly at him. Then it speaks, in a low, slow, and threatening voice:

"GET. THAT. CUTE. ROBOT."

The Galactic Authority troops go on alert, each one pulling out a laser pistol and aiming it at C.O.B. Act fast!

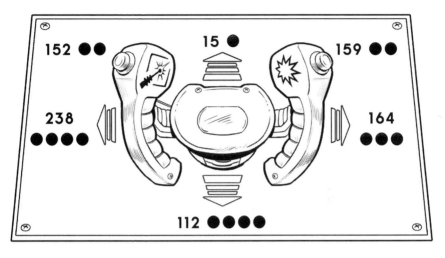

Leaving the graveyard crossroads behind you, you mentally push the joystick forward toward the Crypt Gate. Yes, it's probably pretty foolish to attempt to conquer this stage of the game so soon, but you're a risk-taker. A rebel! And you've played plenty of video games before—how hard could this vintage game that you've never even heard of be, anyway? But if you want to go back, you can always return to the crossroads and choose to move in another direction.

No?

You're going to continue?

Really?

You're SURE about that?

Okay. Fair enough. You keep pushing toward the Crypt Gate, and as you get closer and closer, you can feel something strange in the air. In fact, it IS the air—it's getting colder and colder as you continue. The temperature is dropping rapidly, and by the time you reach the Crypt Gate, you're shivering. It's freezing—literally. All around you are statues that almost look as if they are made of ice, and some of them look suspiciously like statues of adventurers. Icicles hang from the eaves of the nearby tombs, the earth and dead grass beneath your feet is crunchy with frost, and before you looms the Crypt Gate, an ornate assembly of cruelly forged iron and wickedly carved stone that, in a word, is TERRIFYING. Its bars are completely covered with thick, dirty ice, and the lock in the middle is a gigantic metal box shaped like a tomb.

You prod the lock with your sword, tapping it to see if you can dislodge any of the ice, but nothing happens. It's frozen solid, and nothing short of a blazing fire is going to break that ice. And still the temperature is dropping. You're not getting through this gate any time soon, and you figure that you should retreat to a warmer part of the graveyard before you freeze to death, so you turn to go back in the direction you came from. But as you do, a chill wind whips up, and snow begins to fall and swirl around you. In moments, the snow coalesces into what looks like the form of a cloaked figure—it's an ice version of the hooded necromancer you saw earlier! It stands before you, at least seven feet tall, and spreads its arms. The monster then speaks, its words sending a chill down your spine.

"You have trespassed in my domain of icy death, and for that I have sent my Abominable Snowmancer to make you pay the ULTIMATE PRICE!" Sounds serious. What do you do?!

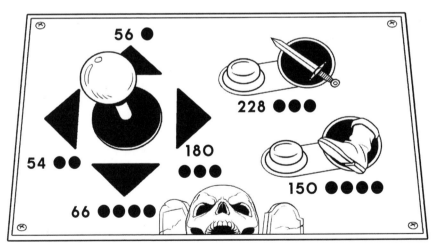

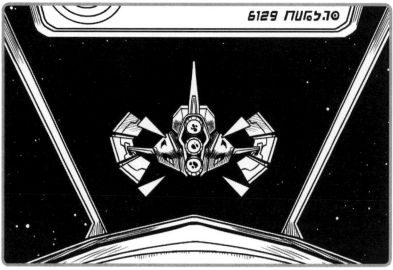

You've figured out which Black Angel is the real one, and now you have it in your sights. There's nothing left to do but finish the job. What's your plan?

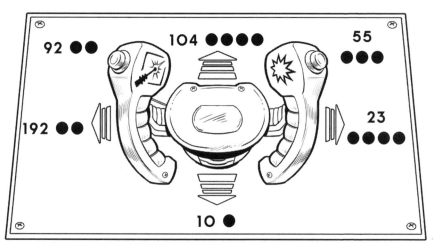

●

You jump in place, feeling the gradual development and strengthening of your leg muscles. Exercise is a good habit. Keep it up (but jumping in place doesn't take you forward, so choose a direction to travel).

Head back to 76 ●●●

●●

C.O.B. turns toward the screen, presses a button on his robotic wrist, and then snaps off another salute. *Gee, that stealth bot is cute*, you think, right before he turns into a ball of white light.

Head to 71 ●●●

⬤⬤⬤

You pull back on your control yoke to climb.

"Slow down there, Cadet," you hear Sgt. Brixto say. "We're almost ready to scrap. Patience." Heeding the wisdom of your superior officer, you relax your grip on the controls and let your spacecraft level out.

Head back to 129 ⬤

⬤⬤⬤⬤

Perhaps leaping about will confuse this creature, you think. You do so, and in mid-leap it extends its broadsword and neatly cuts you in half. Fair's fair.

YOU ARE DEAD. CONTINUE: Y/N?
Y: Head to 167 ⬤ N: Head to 242 ⬤⬤

You turn to the left, and the Galactic Authority fighter narrowly misses colliding with you . . . and starts firing at you! Before you can successfully evade its blasts, you are caught in a hail of lasers and, well, get blown to smithereens.

YOU ARE DEAD. CONTINUE: Y/N?
Y: Head to 129 ⬤ N: Head to 242 ⬤⬤

●●

You move forward and fall off the Skele-King to your death on the stones below. Ow!

YOU ARE DEAD. CONTINUE: Y/N?
Y: Head to 167 ● **N: Head to 242** ●●●

●●●

You turn your controls to the right, and as you do, the other Black Angel disappears from view. You're chasing the right one, and it's doing everything it can to get away. But you persist, and in moments, your targeting guide passes over it . . . and flashes! You've got the Black Angel dead to rights!

Head to 158 ●●●●

●●●●

You move to your right, just avoiding the teeth of the biting skull and then dodging as the sightless skeleton body clumsily attempts to slash and impale you with its sword. But you hadn't counted on the skeleton sticking out its leg and tripping you, causing you to fall through the open door of the nearest tomb. Before you can get up, the skeleton reaches out and pulls the door to the tomb shut! You pound on the heavy stone slab, but nobody—and no THING—comes to your aid. Prepare for eternity, because . . .

YOU ARE DEAD. CONTINUE: Y/N?
Y: Head to 167 ● N: Head to 242 ●●●

●

Sword in hand, you head through the graveyard, toward the gate that leads to the mysterious Castle-Crypt—which, if what you saw when you climbed to the top of the tomb was any indication, is the lair of some heavy-duty necromancer type. Come to think of it, he'd be the type of bad dude who would probably be the final boss in any regular video game. Are you ready to face him? Dismissing the thought, you continue forward, jumping over tombstones in your way and occasionally striking old statuary with your sword, reducing the busts and urns to dust. Sadly, you never find any power-ups or new weapons in the debris.

Soon, you come to a crossroads in the graveyard. Ahead of you, the path to the north gate continues. To the west is the narrow avenue to the Village Gate, which looks to be difficult terrain, as it's strewn with the rubble of graves that look as if they've been cracked apart and ransacked by hundreds of years of tomb raids.

To the east, you can just barely make out the path to the Swamp Gate, as a miasmic-looking fog seems to have settled among the tombstones, obscuring the view. And behind you is the path that you've just come up.

Which way do you go?

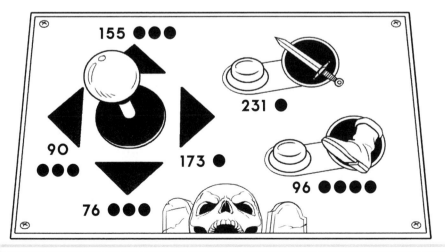

155 ●●●

90
●●●

173 ●

76 ●●●

231 ●

96 ●●●●

●●

You try to feint to the left, but the skeleton is too quick and blocks your path.

Head back to 184 ●

●●●

You make C.O.B. run to the right, a move which confuses the Spider-Bots that follow him. But shaking them means that you have run him directly into the Galactic Authority troops' line of fire. He's struck multiple times and comes skidding to a halt, his body half-melted. The battery face . . . smiles.

"TAKE. THAT. CUTE. ROBOT. HA. HA. HA. HA. NOW. LET'S. GET. BACK. TO. WORK. AND. DESTROY. SOME. SPACE. PIRATES."

It's not bad enough that you failed in your mission. No, you had to hear that weird battery-face thing gloating about it, too. What a way to find out that it's the end.

Head to 242 ●●●

●●●●

You dodge to the right, hoping to avoid the heat of the Death-King's fearsome blast, but unfortunately the undead tyrant seems to have sensed your plan, sweeping its hands to follow you. This time you aren't quick enough to escape the beam of destruction, and you are swiftly and handily disintegrated until you are reduced to yet more dust to decorate this decrepit place. Bummer.

Head to 242 ●●●

●

You try evasive action in a desperate attempt to avoid the terrible gaze of Slaystation Omega, but it SEES you. You climb, you dive, you bank to the left and to the right, but its gaze follows you, inexorably, ultimately catching up to your ship and breaking it (and you) into a million pieces.

Head to 242 ●●●

●●

Taking evasive action, you bank to the left, hoping to buy some time and figure out what the heck is going on here, but as your ship collides head-on with a Galactic Authority ship, you finally understand what Sgt. Brixto was getting at when he said "coming in hot from nine and twelve o'clock."

YOU ARE DEAD. CONTINUE: Y/N?
Y: Head to 129 ● N: Head to 242 ●●●

●●●

Fearlessly you move TOWARD the Death-King's deadly bolt of dark energy, and fearlessly you are instantly reduced to nothing more than ashes. Next time, at least make an effort and use a shield! Sheesh.

Head to 242 ●●●

You are now at the controls of a tough-as-nails Tank Walker with Galactic Authority troops aiming to take you down.

What's your move?

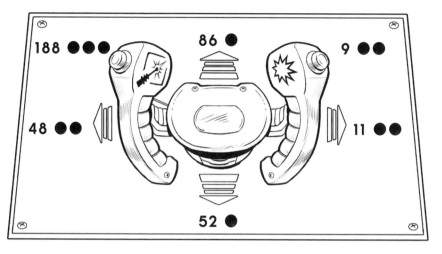

●

Feeling drawn to the monstrous medieval adventure promised by *Crypt Quest*, you approach the machine as it plays spooky, minor-key music.

"Enter my graveyard—and DIE!" says a sepulchral voice emanating from the cabinet, followed by sinister laughter. Gulping, you drop your token into the coin slot and press the Start button. As soon as you do, a green mist begins to seep out from under the *Crypt Quest* cabinet, coiling around your feet and filling the Midnight Arcade until you can see nothing around you, nothing at all.

Wind stirs the green mist, causing it to loop in spooky, silent whorls, and when it clears, you see that you are no longer in the Midnight Arcade—you're standing in what looks to be an ancient cemetery; paths enclosed by broken crypts and lined with cobblestones and weeds lead forward and to your right and left. Looking down at yourself, you see that you're now dressed in some kind of armor, and you're unarmed.

What's happening here? you wonder. *Where AM I?*

You turn around and see that you're on one side of a gigantic wrought iron gate in the tall stone wall that looks as if it borders the graveyard. You grab the gate with both of your hands and try to open it, shaking it, but it's locked tight by a massive, rusty padlock. Looking up at the arch over the gate, you see this carved into its stone:

And that's when you figure it out: Somehow, someway, you're INSIDE the *Crypt Quest* game, and to get out of this strange place, you're going to have to think of this as a GAME and PLAY your way out. And to do that, you must first figure out the rules of this strange place. Suddenly an image flashes before you, an image of the joystick and action buttons of the *Crypt Quest* game back in the Midnight Arcade. That's the key—you have to think like the controller. You know instinctually that most of the decisions you will make while trapped in this game world will be based on these controls. If you recall correctly, the controls for *Crypt Quest* were fairly basic, like this:

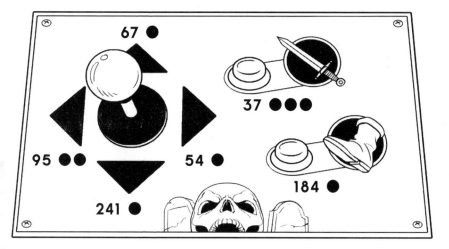

So: What would you like to do?

●●

You fall off the Skele-King and hit the ground. *Crunch!*

YOU ARE DEAD. CONTINUE: Y/N?

Y: Head to 167 ●   N: Head to 242 ●●●

●●●

You push your ship into a shallow dive, hoping to keep on the Black Angel's tail, but your enemy has pulled up, causing you to lose sight of them! You look around frantically, but no—there's nothing out there. How did the Black Angel completely disappear? Was it a cloaking device of some sort?

And then, as if to answer your question, the nothingness of outer space in front of you shimmers, and the Black Angel appears ahead of you, headed directly toward you, lasers firing.

So, yes, it WAS a cloaking device. How about that?

YOU ARE DEAD. CONTINUE: Y/N?

Y: Head to 43 ●●●   N: Head to 242 ●●●

●●●●

Pulling your arm from Sgt. Brixto's grasp, you join the rush of Space Pirates who are heading toward the starship hangar, rushing into another dogfight with the forces of the Galactic Authority.

"Cadet!" you hear Sgt. Brixto yell as he gets caught in the crowd. "I mean, Corporal. Lieutenant! You're needed this way, come this wayyyyyyy . . ." But the rest of the sergeant's words are lost in the hubbub, and you're too excited about the prospect of battle against the mysterious Slaystation Omega to care.

In moments, you and the rest of the Space Pirates reach the hangar, where dozens of battle-scarred space fighters are in various stages of action. Alarms are still clanging and buzzing, but even in the mad confusion, you feel a singular sense of purpose among your fellow Space Battlers. You're all in this together, and you feel like you can win this thing.

You locate an unassigned space fighter and climb into its now-familiar cockpit, the controls feeling like old friends. Wasting no time, you signal to the dispatcher that you're ready to take off and join the fray, and in seconds you're zooming off into the void of space.

Once again, you join a group of fighters, and you all

trade jocular taunts and reassurances over the comms link. It all seems A-OK . . . until you see IT.

Slaystation Omega, dead ahead.

It's larger than it looked on Sgt. Brixto's screen. Much larger. And scarier. Much, much scarier.

There's silence over the comms link as you and the rest of the crew scream toward the fearsome space juggernaut. Nobody's joking now.

And then, the EYES of Slaystation Omega open. They're bright, dancing with energy, and before you can process what's going on, BEAMS OF DEADLY FORCE shoot from the eyes, tearing the ships of your unsuspecting allies asunder. Its gaze shifts, and the beams move . . . toward you!

SLAYSTATION OMEGA is trying to destroy you. What do you do? We repeat: What. Do. You. Do?

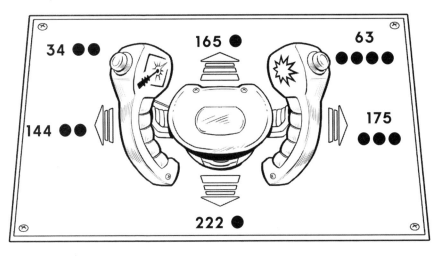

34 ●●

165 ●

63 ●●●●

144 ●●

175 ●●●

222 ●

●

You move toward the icky mist that seems to be emanating from the swamp. Soon, it surrounds you, wrapping around your ankles in sticky, humid tendrils that almost feel solid. As you get closer to the Swamp Gate, the air becomes heavier and warmer, and you can see that vines and other plants are growing all over the graves in this part of the graveyard, slowly breaking them apart into crumbling ruins. You also see bones and skulls among the vines, as if the vegetation has been pulling corpses from the graves for some sinister, plant-y purpose.

Eventually you arrive at the graveyard's east gate, which is much like the gate you first appeared by, only this one is thoroughly overgrown with wicked-looking swamp vines. You move closer to the gate and peer through its bars: Beyond it lies a fetid, evil-looking swamp. Trees with drooping branches rise from the water and crowd together, creating a canopy over a narrow path that leads away from the gate. It's dark out there in the swamp, and you think you see . . . things moving back there among the trees. Things with more than two legs. You can't be quite sure, though, and when you try to open the gate, it's held closed tight not only by the vines but also by an iron lock, which is so overgrown with mold and vegetation and a thick coating of swamp slime that even if you had the key, it'd be impossible to spring the thing open.

You're facing the gate, and to your left and right, there are paths that border the graveyard's wall that lead toward the north and south. You begin to mentally picture the *Crypt Quest* controls, but something strange begins to happen. The vines inside the gate and around you begin to curl and twist together, almost as if some sort of intelligence is making them move. And it's not just the vines—they're carrying bones from the graves around you, pulling them all together into one weird mass, a creature that's part plant and part bone—a Hortiskull!

Head to 136 ●●

●●

Figuring that the best defense is a good offense, you rush the Death-King, hoping to defeat the beast in hand-to-hand combat. But with a cryptic, arcane gesture, the evil enchanter causes the ground beneath your feet to crumble! Before you can avoid the trap, you fall into the newly made hole, the Death-King's laughter following you as you keep falling down, down, down, down . . .

Head to 242 ●●●

●●●

You try evasive action in a desperate attempt to avoid the terrible gaze of Slaystation Omega, but it SEES you. You climb, you dive, you bank to the left and to the right, but its gaze follows you, inexorably, ultimately catching up to your ship and breaking it (and you) into a million pieces.

Head to 242 ●●●

●●●●

You've escaped from living vines and managed to outwit an earthquake, so it's with immense satisfaction that you look at your map and discover that, yes indeed, you are close to your destination. Your Walker trudges on through the thick jungle, and you are on alert for whatever this hellscape can throw at you next. Could it be volcanoes? Quicksand? Creatures thirsting for your blood? All three? It's possible. And then you hear it again—that strange and chilling howl off in the distance, seemingly uttered by some of the native fauna of this planet. Whatever it is, you hope you never meet it, because it sounds nasty. Shaking your negative thoughts from your head, you pilot your Walker along the path on the map, getting closer to the base with every step.

Finally, your Walker emerges from the jungle, and you find yourself at your destination: You've reached the Space Pirates outpost! It's a small base comprising a few buildings, and it seems like it used to be tidy and efficient but that many years have passed since anyone last visited this place; the vines of the jungle—the NON-sentient ones, apparently—have begun to take over, creeping over structures and slowly working their way into the buildings' guts, beginning the process of tearing them down and reclaiming the land. But landscaping issues aside, what you see a few hundred meters ahead cheers you up immensely: It's a launchpad, upon which is the rocket booster that's your ticket back into orbit, back to the Space Pirates. You're getting closer to beating this game. Cautiously, you edge the Walker forward toward the rocket.

And that's when you hear it: An unearthly yowl comes from the jungle just beyond the launchpad, sending birds flying in all directions. It's a screaming challenge that sounds like it was voiced by a hundred mutant apes assembled in a glee club. The trees where the yell came from start to thrash back and forth, as if something HUGE is moving them aside. Something bigger than you.

And then it emerges from the tree line, and whatever you THOUGHT it was going to be, it's much, much worse. The monster looks like a nightmare combination of a dinosaur and a gorilla, and it stands more than two stories tall. It moves to stand in front of the rocket and stares at you with its four very mean eyes. Then it raises its arms and cries out again. The cry is in no language that you understand, but its meaning is clear: "Get off my turf," it says.

Uh-oh. This isn't good. Not at all.

As you and the behemoth stand there facing each other, Sgt. Brixto's face once again appears on your screen.

"Corporal! You're alive!" the alien says. "That's incredible! And great. Yeah, that too. How do you do it? I'm tracking you right now, and it looks like you've reached the base. Well, strap your Walker into that rocket and get yer can up here. Things are coming to a head, and we need every hand we can muster. What are you waiting for?"

You quickly explain to Sgt. Brixto that a gigantic . . . gorilla-dinosaur thing stands between you and your escape. He shakes his head.

"Yeah, argh. THOSE things. 'Gorillosaurs' we used to call 'em. Real creative on our part, I know. Mean bunch of critters. Lost a lot of good Space Pirates to them. They're actually one of the reasons we abandoned that base. Tough neighborhood, if you catch my drift. Well, if you . . ."

But you don't hear the rest of what Sgt. Brixto has to say, because that's when the Gorillosaur decides that it's had enough of waiting and charges toward you!

Head to 68 ●●●●

You try to use your special weapon, but nothing happens. Why did they install this button if it doesn't DO anything?

A Galactic Authority fighter is zooming directly toward you, at speed. Think quick!

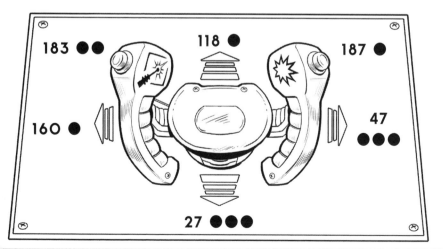

●●

Thinking that perhaps the Galactic Authority pilot has another slick move up their sleeve, you put your ship into a dive. You've chosen wrong, however, and the fighter you were pursuing does a loop and a barrel roll, suddenly pursuing YOU, and in an instant you have been reduced to space ash . . .

YOU ARE DEAD. CONTINUE: Y/N?
Y: Head to 129 ● N: Head to 242 ●●●

●●●

You lunge to the right, hoping to put the Abominable Snowmancer behind you and reach the Swamp Gate, but with a gesture, the snowbound sorcerer makes a wall of ice and snow in front of you, foiling your plan. You collide with the wall and fall to the ground, stunned, and as you try to collect your wits, you feel the creature touching you, and your body is instantly frozen solid. You shouldn't have come this direction so woefully unprepared because now . . .

YOU ARE DEAD. CONTINUE: Y/N?
Y: Head to 167 ● N: Head to 242 ●●●

Slashing your sword, you strike the well cover, splintering its rotted wood and sending shards falling down into the well's depths. Peering down into the stygian darkness, you hear the echo of the debris hitting the sides of the well, then, after what seems like an eternity, hitting the surface of water far below. Feeling pretty glad you didn't jump on the cover and fall to your death, you're about to walk away when you hear a VOICE come out of the well, a voice that's faint, almost as if it were miles away, or as if this was an Almost-Bottomless Well. The voice chants these words in a singsong rhythm:

> *Your Crypt Quest now has just begun.*
>
> *If you don't die, you'll have some fun.*
>
> *Now you must seek another key*
>
> *If you hope to escape with ease.*

As the last word echoes up out of the well, something isn't sitting right with you. Then you put your finger on it and shout down the well.

"Hey—'key' doesn't rhyme with 'ease.'"

"Yes, it does," says the voice from the Almost-Bottomless Well, sounding a little bit snotty and annoyed.

"No, it doesn't."

"Well, it's close enough," the voice retorts. "Yeesh. Anyway, why are you wasting time critiquing expository fantasy poems when you have a Crypt Quest to complete? Leave me alone."

And with that, the gate on the left of the plaza swings open. Beyond it you can see a narrow, shadowy avenue leading farther into the village. But the gate on the right remains closed. Strange. As you stand there, you puzzle over the inane verse for a few moments, wondering if hidden in its four brief lines was some sort of clue about how to beat the game, besides finding another key . . .

Nope. You've got nothing.

"Good luck!" says the voice from the Almost-Bottomless Well, before adding at a lower volume, "You're gonna neeeed iiiiit . . ."

When you're ready to go down the path on your left, head to 115 ●

●

You try to feint to the left, but the Skele-King brings down its enormous broadsword, forcing you to reconsider.

Head back to 206 ●●●

●●

PSHEW! PSHEW! The lasers of your space fighter arc out into the darkness of space . . . and score a direct hit! The Galactic Authority ship disintegrates into a ball of flame and debris that you blow through unscathed. "Yes!" yells Sgt. Brixto over the comms link. "Let's go get 'em, Cadet!"

Head to 69 ●

●●●

The locked graveyard gate blocks your way, and why would you want to leave, anyway? Adventure lies ahead!

Head back to 76 ●●●

●●●●

Well, as it turns out, the ground ALL AROUND YOU is crumbling, including the space you just set foot on. Arms windmilling wildly, you try to stay upright, but there's nothing there . . .

Head to 242 ●●●

●

Jumping up, you grab the top of the nearest tomb and pull yourself up to its roof. What better way to figure out what's going on than to survey your surroundings? As you look around, what you see astounds you: You are in a walled graveyard, and hundreds of graves, tombstones, and mausoleums surround you in every direction. You are at the south end of the necropolis. Beyond the gate that stands at the graveyard's west entrance, you can see what looks to be an abandoned village. To the east, a gate leads to what appears to be a noxious swamp. And beyond the gate to the north, there sits a crumbling castle, silhouetted in the moonlight. It's imposing and frightening. It looks like a gigantic crypt. Suddenly, above the strange and fearsome structure, a hooded face appears, like a magical projection on the clouds, and two red eyes underneath the hood seem to look directly at you . . . into your very soul.

"Enter my domain—and DIE!" the hooded figure says, laughing maniacally before it fades away into nothingness. Out of nowhere, a chill wind of terrific strength begins to blow, so fierce that it blows you off the top of the tomb and back down to where you began. *This is impossible*, you think. But as the thought crosses your mind, you hear the sound of the earth being disturbed: A few feet in front of you, a skeleton wearing a rusty suit of armor and carrying a short but effective-looking sword is clawing its way out of a nearby sarcophagus.

Seeing you, the skeleton begins to advance, skeletal fingers grasping. It's time for some action, and once again you picture the controller for *Crypt Quest* in your mind. So: Faced with undead peril . . . What's your move?

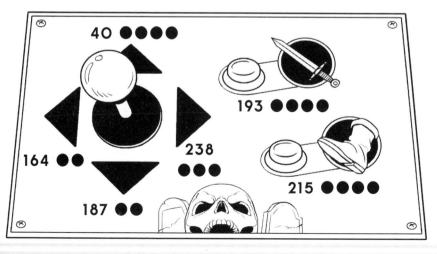

●●

The Stone-King strikes, and as it does, you once again try to evade its attack with a nimble leap. This time, however, your luck has run out. It's figured out your scheme and catches you mid–nimble leap. We don't have the heart to describe what happens next. Let's just say that . . .

YOU ARE DEAD. CONTINUE: Y/N?
Y: Head to 196 ●● N: Head to 242 ●●●

●●●

You pull back on the control yoke, and your ship's engines begin to whir. For a moment, you almost have liftoff, and you rise a few feet . . . and then crash back to the ground. The power in the ship cuts off abruptly. All systems are dead, and nothing's responding. Pounding on the controls with frustration, you look up and see the hover tank enter the clearing, aiming its laser weapon directly at you. It fires at the cockpit, and . . .

YOU ARE DEAD. CONTINUE: Y/N?
Y: Head to 56 ●● N: Head to 242 ●●●

●●●●

Figuring that a good offense is your best defense, you swing your sword at the Skele-King, only to have it block your strike with a swing of its fearsome broadsword. The impact of your two blades colliding is so powerful that it knocks out one of your fillings.

Head back to 206 ●●●

●

What the hey? This thing just doesn't seem to work. No matter how many times you press it, you get nothing, zilch, nada. Is it there for decoration? Just to tease you? Or did the mechanics back at the base forget to repair it? Any way you look at it, it's a bust.

"Quit messing around with that thing," Sgt. Brixto says.

Head to 69 ●

●●

You retreat as the skeleton moves toward you, but before you can go very far, your back hits the massive iron gate, and no matter how hard you push against it, it won't budge. And still the skeleton gets closer to you . . .

Head back to 184 ●

● ● ●

You fire your lasers, and the Galactic Authority troops scramble as they run for cover. Unfortunately, your laser fire bounces harmlessly off the hover tank's armor. In response to your attack, the hover tank aims its cannon at you . . . and fires! Its projectile packs a wallop, and even though it doesn't kill you, it knocks you backward into a tree, causing it to crack and fall.

Head to 141 ● ● ● ●

● ● ● ●

You bounce up and down on the Skele-King's shoulders, which annoys it but does nothing else. Choose again.

Head back to 49 ● ● ● ●

●

Carefully you put the Skeleton Key that you won from the Skele-King into the skull-shaped lock that holds the gate shut. Much to your surprise, the old mechanisms within the lock turn with ease, and the lock snaps open with a crack. On their own, the gates to the Abandoned Village creak open, and, senses alert, you cautiously creep inside and stand in its empty plaza.

And as soon as you do, the air before you shimmers with dark energy, and an apparition appears: The hooded figure you saw earlier hovers above the plaza, its red eyes looking directly at you. A sinister chuckle emanates from beneath its hood, echoing off the stone and wood of the village plaza.

"Enter the village . . . AND DIE!" booms the creature's bone-chilling voice. Before you even realize what you're doing, you're charging toward it and raising your sword to strike. But the malevolent spirit fades away before you can connect, and your blade cuts only through the air. *Whatever that strange thing is*, you think, *I'm going to have to fight it soon. But how?*

Your grim thoughts are interrupted when you hear the gates to the Abandoned Village begin to creak again: They're closing, moving at the behest of some strange force that you can't see! You rush to grab them and hold them open, but whatever is pulling them closed is too strong and drags you with the gates, even as you dig your heels into the cobblestones.

Clang! The gates come together with a decisive clank of metal upon metal. You spend a few moments trying to forcefully pull them open, but they won't budge.

Looking around, you note that you're standing in

a small, semicircular plaza, the entrance to a once-prosperous village that is now devoid of life. Nothing stirs here, and an eerie, almost oppressive SILENCE surrounds you. Directly in front of you is a disused well, sealed by a wooden cover. To your right and left, you can see two twisty lanes that lead deeper into the shadows cast by the decrepit, leaning buildings of stone and thatch, but each one of them is blocked by a wooden gate. A third lane is straight ahead, but it's completely barricaded by what looks to be the rubble of a collapsed building.

Just like in the graveyard, you know that soon you'll be facing strange, supernatural threats as you try to find the key that will open the next gate, the one that will lead to the next level. But what gruesome form will these new foes take?

You're locked inside the Abandoned Village and have to figure out how to get to the next level. What's your move?

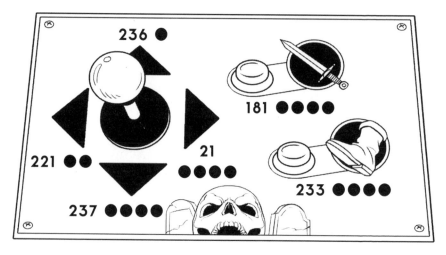

Seriously? You've got the Black Angel in your crosshairs and you blow it breaking off in another direction? Have you ever heard the phrase "Snatching defeat from the jaws of victory"? Well, you have now! You probably deserve what happens next, which is piloting your ship directly into a hail of enemy fire. Alas!

YOU ARE DEAD. CONTINUE: Y/N?
Y: Head to 43 ●●● N: Head to 242 ●●●

You take your sword's hilt in both hands and aim the blade toward the center of the Skele-King's skull, and . . .

Head to 139 ●●●

●●●●

As the skeletal warrior gets closer, you decide that you have nothing else to lose and PUNCH it full-force in the chest, a blow which sends it reeling backward and causes it to fall to the ground, its skull detaching from its body in the process. But it's not "dead" yet—the skeleton reaches out for its missing head, patting the ground frantically for where it thinks it might be. It's only a matter of moments until it finds its head and attacks again.

What's your move?

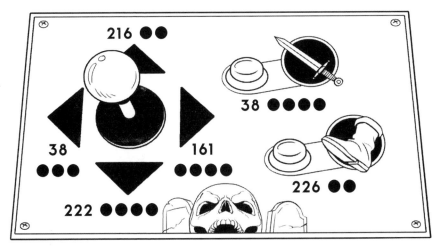

●

You back away from the Skele-King, only to find
yourself hopelessly STUCK. The Skele-King turns to see
you struggling, and if a skeleton could smile, this one
certainly would as it reaches toward you . . .

YOU ARE DEAD. CONTINUE: Y/N?
Y: Head to 167 ● N: Head to 242 ●●●

●●

The wild Gorillosaur stands before you, eyeing your
Walker mech warily, hunching over and breathing
heavily. It looks like it's about to attack again, but it's
waiting to see what your next move is. Then, it stands up
straight, beats its chest, and lets loose its unearthly howl.

So: What's your next move?

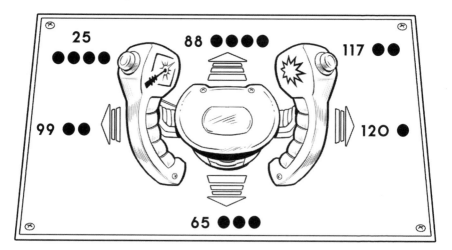

●●●

Timing it just right, you let the fireball get closer . . . closer . . . closer . . . and then you leap over the Death-King's infernal projectile as it almost gets TOO close! Landing deftly on your feet, you turn to watch it as it roars back toward whence you came. Congratulating yourself on your agility and perfect timing, you turn back to the matter at hand and follow the Death-King farther into the castle.

Head to 62 ●●●

●●●●

As the chandeliers crash to the ground, you move to the side of the hall, a strategy that proves to be a mistake, as the now-living monstrous tapestries whip out toward you with uncanny speed, wrapping you up snugly and giving you a close-up view of the horrifying moving creatures trapped within the weave . . .

Head to 242 ●●●

●

Any movement you make seems to send an alert to whatever strange intelligence controls the vines, causing them to squeeze your Walker tighter and slither up your body with even more speed. You pull the controls back, push them forward, and yank them to the right and to the left, but the vines continue to move and squeeze, until you are a vine-wrapped Walker mech mummy. Cracks appear in your cockpit's canopy, and the vines put more and more pressure on it, and then . . .

CRASH! The canopy breaks open, and the vines move IN.

YOU ARE DEAD. CONTINUE: Y/N?
Y: Head to 56 ●● N: Head to 242 ●●●

●●

Your excitement mounts as you climb the last few stairs and emerge back into the plaza of the Abandoned Village. The Flame Key is still warm in your hand, and its warmth seems to travel from your hand, down your arm, and throughout your body, giving you a sense of safety and security. You know that you still have some challenges to beat in this game, but you feel as though you're on the right track. Yes!

Running up to the gate to the graveyard, you attempt to fit the key into the lock, but it's not working. The key won't turn at all.

"Ahem. Having some problems? Perhaps I can help."

It's the voice from the well. You turn and walk over to the lip of the well.

"The gate won't open because the Flame Key opens the north gate of the cemetery, the frozen one. Duh. *This* gate opens after you finish a task. Can you guess what task that is?"

As if on cue, the rubble of the buildings that blocks the center lane in the plaza starts to shift. Bricks fall but then move together and start STACKING on top of one another, joined by wooden beams and cobblestones. Soon, what used to be a pile of trash has reorganized itself into a colossus made of stone!

"Meet the Stone-King," says the voice from the well with no small amount of snark. "Nice knowing you!"

Another level, another miniboss! To go further in the Crypt Quest, you must defeat the Stone-King. It's your move!

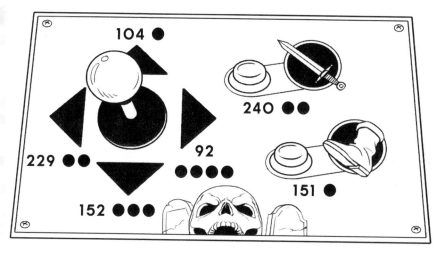

Parched? Hungry? Well, the chances of this place having anything to quench your thirst or sate your hunger are slim to none, but nothing ventured, nothing gained, so you decide to enter and investigate . . .

Head to 63 ●

Lasers are about as effective against an earthquake as you might think, and if you think that's "not effective at ALL," then you are 100 percent correct. So it is with great sadness that you discover this fact as you shoot at an earthquake. The earthquake doesn't seem to notice. In fact, it responds to your assault the only way it knows how, and that's to open up a chasm directly beneath the feet of your Walker. You fall into the new hole, shooting lasers all the way . . .

YOU ARE DEAD. CONTINUE: Y/N?
Y: Head to 56 ●● N: Head to 242 ●●●

●

You jump . . . and you collide with a falling chandelier, sending you sprawling to the ground as the rest of the chandeliers fall—*CRASH! CRASH! CRASH!*—smothering you beneath them. You were nimble, you were quick, but now you're buried under a pile of candlesticks.

Head to 242 ●●●

●●

Swinging your sword to and fro, you manage to deflect the chandeliers as they crash to the ground. But the Death-King is getting away, and the tapestries and the organ look as if they're thirsty for your flesh. Try something else!

Head back to 222 ●●

●●●

You fall backward off the Skele-King's shoulders. You
might have meant to do that, but still . . .

YOU ARE DEAD. CONTINUE: Y/N?
Y: Head to 167 ● **N: Head to 242** ●●

●●●●

Returning to the plaza at the entrance to the village,
you immediately notice that something has changed.
The well in the center of the plaza is still uncovered, the
rubble blocking the center path is still there, and the gate
to the graveyard is still closed, but the wooden gate on
the right is now OPEN. It seems as if finding that soda
machine was the key to unraveling this mystery.

"Hey. Good job!" says the voice from the well. "You
found the soda machine. Excellent."

"Er, thanks," you respond as you head toward the new
opening.

"Say, you didn't happen to save any, did you? The
soda? If you did, could you just pour some down here?
Please? I hear it's great."

You shake the can of Midnight Cola in your hand.
Empty. Shrugging, you dangle it over the well for a
moment and then let go. You wait . . . and wait . . . and

wait . . . and then you hear the can hit the water with a distant *splash.*

"Awwwww. This is EMPTY! C'mon! Go get another one and pour it down here. Please? I mean . . ."

The voice from the well's complaints following you, you decide to head down the right-hand path.

Unlike the left-hand path, the right-hand path seems to be some sort of stairway that winds and twists as it descends. This appears to have formerly been some sort of crafts district before whatever calamity befell this village, for the vacant shops on either side of you advertise their expertise in various types of skilled artisanship. You try the handles on several doors, but everything is locked tight, and as you travel downward, you notice that the temperature is slowly but surely rising. At first, it's just a slight increase in warmth, but soon you're sweating and thinking about shedding your armor for some relief. You know, however, that that's a HORRIBLE idea, and wiping the perspiration from your brow, you keep following the staircase wherever it's leading you.

Soon, you come to the last step and find yourself in another cul-de-sac, but unlike the one in the other part of the village, there is only one place of business here, and it seems to be quite active. At one end of the dead end is an open blacksmith shop with a sign that reads "Gobblo's Smithy" above its door, and in front of the shop there's a fire pit raging, next to which is an anvil. Working in front of the fire is a goblin blacksmith. This, you think, must be Gobblo. You wait and watch Gobblo work, but the goblin doesn't seem to sense your presence. As you stand there, you see him take the mold he's holding over the fire to his anvil and then strike it, opening the mold to reveal an ornate key that is still on fire!

Gobblo finally pauses and looks up at you, without changing his expression.

"So you made it, eh?" Gobblo mutters. "Usually your type doesn't make it past the Skele-King, if you even make it that far. Well, good job. Guess you're going to need this."

Gobblo picks up the flaming key from his anvil and immediately begins to bat it from hand to hand.

"Ooh! Ooh! Ow, ow, ow! Hot, hot, hot! Here you go!"

He tosses the flaming key your way, and even though it's on fire, you reflexively catch it. Expecting it to burn your hand, you're surprised that it feels cool to the touch, even though, yes, it's still on fire. Realizing that you're just fine, you gaze at the magical key in your hand.

CONGRATULATIONS! YOU HAVE ACQUIRED

THE FLAME KEY!

Now Gobblo's impressed. "Drank yourself one of those sodas, I see. Well, good for you. I was expecting you to throw that key as far as you could as fast as you could. Maybe you're finally the one who's got the right stuff to . . . well, we'll see. Anyway—off with you. Back up those stairs!"

And with that, Gobblo actually WINKS at you before going back to the anvil. Knowing when you've been dismissed, you head back up the stairs, Flame Key in hand.

Head to 196 ●●

●

Using your sword, you chop and stab at the vines that

make up the body of the Hortiskull, and at first it seems as if you're making progress, but you soon notice that as soon as you sever any of the stalks, they grow back with magical quickness, reinforcing their horticultural hold. You realize that this is not going to work—your weapon isn't strong enough. As soon as you realize that, the Hortiskull seems to read your mind and retreats beyond the bars of the gate, back into the swamp. It's going to be waiting for you. Attempt something else.

Head back to 136 ●●

●●

Any movement you make seems to send an alert to whatever strange intelligence controls the vines, causing them to squeeze your Walker tighter and slither up your body with even more speed. You pull the controls back, push them forward, and yank them to the right and to the left, but the vines continue to move and squeeze, until you are a vine-wrapped Walker mech mummy. Cracks appear in your cockpit's canopy and the vines put more and more pressure on it, and then . . .

CRASH! The canopy breaks open, and the vines move IN.

YOU ARE DEAD. CONTINUE: Y/N?

Y: Head to 56 ●● N: Head to 242 ●●●

You decide that you need to know who you're standing on, so you brush aside the dirt that obscures the name of the grave's occupant. Eventually, you reveal these words carved into the stone:

LORD TIBIAN THE FIRST

ALL HAIL THE SKELE-KING!

It's not until the ground starts rumbling beneath you that you realize you read those words aloud, and by doing so you've caused something to start happening. Something BAD. The bones around you start hopping up and down as if they're on springs, and strange music begins to fill the air, a tune that sounds almost as if someone is playing its manic melody on a xylophone made of a rib cage, backed up by a synthesizer. The shaking intensifies and almost knocks you over, and you scramble backward to get off the tombstone you're standing on.

As soon as you do, the marble of the tombstone cracks and explodes upward, sending debris flying! Then, two skeletal hands grab the lip of the newly formed hole and pull a skeletal body out of the grave. Unlike the skeleton you faced before, this one is dressed like it used to be someone noble . . . a king, perhaps?

"I am the Skele-King!" it roars. Well, that answers that. "If you want to pass through these gates, the KEY is ME!"

The Skele-King stands before you, wielding its wicked bone broadsword. To get through the gate behind it, you must defeat it in battle. Are you ready? Yes? No? Doesn't matter! What do you do?

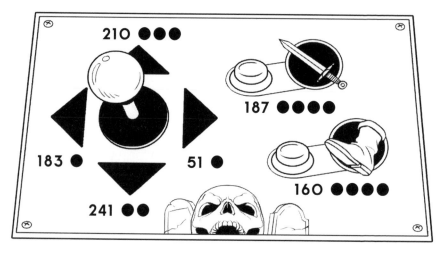

You decide to move toward the strange organ that is somehow playing music by itself, a decision which, it turns out, was not very wise, as the pipes begin to twist and curl like the fingers of an evil, musical hand. Shocked by their animation, you hesitate a moment too long, and that's when they GRAB YOU!

Head to 242 ●●●

●

You decide to see if your special weapon will work on creepy, semi-sentient vines, but nothing happens when you press the button. What else did you expect? At any rate, those are precious seconds you can't get back, and the vines quickly creep up your Walker's body, immobilizing its arms and making it impossible to move. Once you're completely wrapped in your cocoon of evil vegetation, the vines pull, causing you to fall over on your back. Then they pull you again, and you are dragged deep into the jungle, where you see the terrible thing that the vines are attached to . . .

YOU ARE DEAD. CONTINUE: Y/N?
Y: Head to 56 ●● N: Head to 242 ●●●

●●

You're an excellent athlete and can jump very high, like a bounding deer. Choose again.

Turn back to 115 ●

You dash forward just as the Skele-King lunges toward you, ducking through its legs. You are now behind it!

Head to 114

C.O.B. needs no assistance going forward—he's already barreling full speed ahead. Choose another move.

Head back to 4 ●●

You rush to pursue the Death-King in the center but pass through its body—another illusion! You chose poorly, and try to correct your course, but instead find yourself plummeting off a ledge that hangs over a pit of spikes.

Head to 242 ●●●

You move to the right, and all the toys track your movements, turning their well-crafted little heads to keep you dead in their sights. Bizarre, but they aren't attacking. Choose again.

Head back to 64 ●●

●●●

Splintered tree trunk club in your Walker's hand, you survey your surroundings. Smoke pours from the wreckage of the hover tank, and you know that if there was one looking for you, others can't be too far behind. But where can you go? How can you get off this humid rock?

As you wonder, a familiar voice breaks the silence.

"Come in, Cadet. Do you read me? Come in, Cadet! Are you alive? Aw, I think you bought it . . ."

Looking at your view screen, you see the familiar and welcome face of Sgt. Brixto, who's looking back at you with relief and surprise.

"You ARE alive! How did ya manage that?" The sergeant turns his attention to a readout, and comprehension dawns on his face. "Ah, I see—you figured out how to access the Walker mode on your ship. Very clever, Cadet. Or, should I say, Corporal. Congratulations on your field promotion. That sure was some inspired flying you did up here." At that, the sergeant snaps off a salute, which you return.

"Okay, you're safe—for now. But you're not out of the jungle yet. Literally. We need to get you off that planet and back up here to help us destroy the Galactic

Authority once and for all. Time's running out, and rumor has it that they've got some sort of super-ship on its way to wipe us out. We can't defeat them without you, but we can't spare a drop ship to come pick you up, so you're on your own. You need to pilot that Walker through the jungle and to an old Space Pirates outpost. There's a rocket booster there waiting for you. All you've got to do is get to it, attach it to your Walker, and take off. Sending you the coordinates now."

A map appears on the screen, showing a route to the outpost. It looks fairly straightforward, you think. You should be able to pilot your Walker there in no time.

"I know it looks simple, but don't let the map fool you—that planet you're on is a DEATH TRAP. Between the Galactic Authority hunters tracking you, the unmapped natural obstacles, and the native creatures, I don't expect you to make it anywhere near the outpost or see you topside. One false move and you're a goner. But hey, all that aside—good luck! Brixto out."

Somewhere in the distance, out in the depths of the jungle, you hear the cry of an animal. It's a completely wild sound, and whatever made it sounds pretty big and pretty scary. Figuring that there's no time like the present, you glance at the map Sgt. Brixto sent you and, with his "encouragement" still ringing in your ears, you command your Walker to move forward.

After your Walker has been trudging through the jungle steadily for some time, you look at your map and see that you've covered almost a third of the distance to the Space Pirates outpost. Ominous jungle aside, you start thinking that maybe, just maybe, Sgt. Brixto's warnings were a bit over the top. *Maybe he was just trying to encourage me*, you think. Kind of in a weird way, but you can't deny that it's working.

Once again, you hear that strange animal cry in the distance. But this time, it's louder. Whatever it is, it seems to be getting closer. Perhaps whatever's making the sound is following you? You don't want to stick around long enough to find out. You push the Walker forward, picking up the pace a little, when suddenly your motion is stopped. You press forward again on your control yoke, but something's holding you fast. Looking down, you see that your Walker's legs have been captured by a tangle of jungle vines, moving seemingly with a mind of their own!

Your Walker is being attacked by sentient jungle vines!

What do you do?

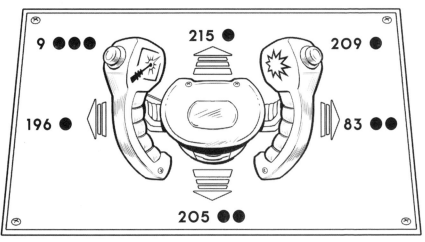

9 ●●●

215 ●

209 ●

196 ●

83 ●●

205 ●●

●●●●

You attempt to climb back up on the tomb in order to escape the skeleton, but as you climb, you feel its creepy digits close around your ankle, grasping you tightly, then pulling you back down to the ground!

Head back to 184 ●

●

Any movement you make seems to send an alert to whatever strange intelligence controls the vines, causing them to squeeze your Walker tighter and slither up your body with even more speed. You pull the controls back, push them forward, and yank them to the right and to the left, but the vines continue to move and squeeze, until you are a vine-wrapped Walker mech mummy. Cracks appear in your cockpit's canopy, and the vines put more and more pressure on it, and then . . .

CRASH! The canopy breaks open, and the vines move IN.

YOU ARE DEAD. CONTINUE: Y/N?
Y: Head to 56 ●● N: Head to 242 ●●●

●●

As you move forward to try to run past the skeleton, the skull starts to hop around like mad, its jaw flapping open and its teeth chattering—it's TALKING to the rest of its body, telling it where you are! The skeleton's arm lashes out faster than you can react and grabs your ankle. As you try to pull away, it holds you tight with its magically strong grip. Then, with its other hand, it stabs its sword at you, and, well, the sword enters you from the front and exits you from the back. As you die in the graveyard, these words begin to flash before your dimming eyes:

YOU ARE DEAD. CONTINUE: Y/N?
Y: Head to 167 ● **N: Head to 242** ●●

●●●

The Death-King leads you on a harrowing chase through the twisting hallways of the Castle-Crypt, taking you farther and farther into its clammy, cold-as-the-grave depths. The path twists and turns, and many times the fleeing form of the Death-King disappears around a corner, and you think you've lost the undead villain. But your senses have been sharpened by your time in the graveyard and the Abandoned Village, and you react to its movements with a sureness that almost feels instinctual. You're figuring out the patterns of this strange game world, and you know that if you just follow your instincts and don't overthink the coming battle, you might have a chance to BEAT *Crypt Quest*.

The Death-King is only steps ahead of you, and you reach out in an attempt to grab the fiend, but with a final burst of speed, the Death-King rounds another corner, just evading your grasp. You turn the corner to follow and see that you've reached a dead end: A vast and decrepit chamber opens before you, its decaying decorations and crumbling furniture clueing you in to its former glory as the throne room of some long-forgotten royalty. But now? Now death rules from the tattered throne on the dais. Or rather, the DEATH-KING rules, for it sits on the throne, and as you rush toward it, it raises a bony palm and you find that you cannot move, your momentum arrested by the weird magic of your nemesis.

"So, you've come this far," the Death-King says with a chilling chuckle. "Past my minions in the graveyard and the Abandoned Village. Truly, you are a talented warrior. But are you a GREAT one? We shall see! Let's FIGHT!"

The Death-King waves its hand, and you feel the bonds of its magic releasing you, freeing you to move once again. But before you can charge forward, sword raised, the Death-King has another trick up its moldering sleeve. It extends both of its arms, throwing a beam of dark energy directly toward you! React . . . now!

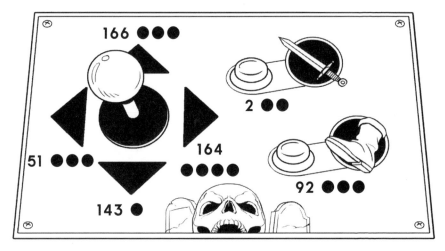

You and the Gorillosaur are locked in hand-to-hand combat! The fearsome face of your foe, all teeth and four eyes of it, is directly in front of you, snarling with hunger. It may not know that it can't eat Walker mechs, but it definitely wants the juicy meat inside of it—that means YOU! So now what?

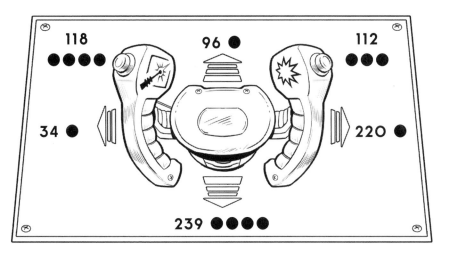

118 ●●●●
96 ●
112 ●●●
34 ●
220 ●
239 ●●●●

●

You're almost at the end of the game, so going back isn't an option. Choose again!

Turn back to 62 ●●●

●●

You swing your sword at the fireball, hoping that it will deflect the missile . . . and it does! Your blade cleaves the fireball in two, but there's no heat—the fireball was a magical concoction, a figment of sorcerous trickery. As the vaporous remnants of the Death-King's illusion curl and dissipate like fog around you, you see that the Death-King has fled down the hall, and you give chase.

Head to 62 ●●●

Okay, here's how this scenario plays out: You press the button, C.O.B. explodes and takes out the Spider-Bots. But here's the thing—you were close to your goal, but not close enough. The Galactic Authority goes on to win the Space Battle, and since it seems that you like losing, you probably know by now that it's the end.

Head to 242 ●●●

●●●●

Thinking that maybe you can buy some time by running down the left path, you break in that direction, only for the Stone-King to snatch you by the collar as you run. It holds you up, opens its mouth, and drops you down its stone gullet.

YOU ARE DEAD. CONTINUE: Y/N?
Y: Head to 196 ●● N: Head to 242 ●●●

●

You pull the Gorillosaur to the side, hoping to knock it off balance, but the agile jungle beast rolls with your motion and FLIPS you over, causing you to crash to the ground. Before you can recover from the jarring reversal, the beast stands over you, places both feet squarely on your body, and TEARS an arm from your Walker! Holding the arm aloft victoriously, it then brings it down . . . and connects, through some strange twist of science-fate, with a circuit inside of your Walker, causing it to blow sky-high, taking the Gorillosaur (who probably died happy) with it.

YOU ARE DEAD. CONTINUE: Y/N?
Y: Head to 68 ●●●● N: Head to 242 ●●●

You try to push open the wooden gate and move down the left lane, but no amount of pushing will open it. It seems as if something—or someONE—doesn't want you to go this way.

Head back to 188 ●

●●●

C.O.B.'s already running that way! Choose again!
Head back to 105 ●●

● ● ● ●

Hey, you've already tried to move that way, and the result is the same: The gate is LOCKED TIGHT. There's no escaping the fiend in this direction. Choose again!

Head back to 193 ● ● ● ●

●

You try evasive action in a desperate attempt to avoid the terrible gaze of Slaystation Omega, but it SEES you. You climb, you dive, you bank to the left and to the right, but its gaze follows you, inexorably, ultimately catching up to your ship and breaking it (and you) into a million pieces.

Head to 242 ● ● ●

● ●

Cautiously you cross the threshold of the Castle-Crypt and enter its main hall. You didn't quite know what to expect, but you might have figured that it would look something like this: Before you is a vast open space lit by torches and hanging chandeliers with dripping candles. Large tapestries that depict weird monsters, demons, ghosts, and other assorted diabolical bad guys hang from the walls on both sides of the room. On the right side of the hall there sits a huge musical instrument that looks like a pipe organ made from the remains of a giant spider. Everything is almost completely covered in frayed cobwebs and ancient dust, as if the castle was decorated by a ghoulish interior designer.

As you marvel at your macabre surroundings, a great gust of air expels clouds of dust from the pipes of the organ, and the keys begin to move on their own. Discordant tones issue from the instrument, like an unseen player is warming up for a grand performance, and, as if on cue, the mysterious hooded figure that's been taunting you throughout *Crypt Quest* appears out of thin air at the far end of the hall. The Death-King! But this time, you can tell it's not simply a phantom—it's REAL. It raises its arms theatrically and then points directly at you.

"Follow me to my throne room and face me—if you DARE!"

Cackling evilly, the Death-King of the Castle-Crypt begins to run away but stops and turns back toward you.

"And DIE!" it adds before continuing to run and disappearing into the darkness beyond with a swirl of its cloak. All is silent for a moment.

Once again, music begins, but this time it's a pulsing,

manic theme that sounds as if it is being played on an infernal computerized harpsichord. The tapestries on the walls begin to undulate, the monsters depicted on them moving and gazing at you with hunger, and the chandeliers above start to sway. You know that this music can only mean one thing: The BOSS BATTLE has begun! What do you do?

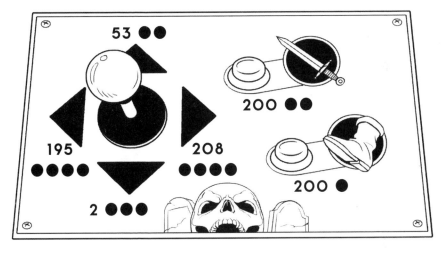

●●●

You advance toward the Hortiskull, and it recoils, spreading its arms as if to protect the gate, before oozing through the bars and slinking away into the swamp. Choose a different tactic.

Head back to 136 ●●

●●●●

You pilot the bot to the left . . . and C.O.B. slides down a ramp in the darkness, the Spider-Bots close behind. After a moment, C.O.B.'s feet find the floor—you've made the right choice! C.O.B. sprints ahead as the Spider-Bots slide down the ramp behind him and continue their relentless chase.

Head to 4 ●●

●

Your Walker once again fires its lasers at the hover tank, and once again your shots bounce harmlessly off, leaving only scorch marks in their wake. Emboldened, the hover tank aims its cannon directly at your Walker . . . and fires. And this time, you aren't merely knocked back, you're cut completely in half! What a way to go.

YOU ARE DEAD. CONTINUE: Y/N?
Y: Head to 56 ●● **N: Head to 242** ●●●

●●

Inspiration strikes you as you watch the skeleton frantically try to grab its skull, and before you can think twice, you decide to STOMP on your prone enemy. Jumping into the air, you aim your feet at the skull, and you immediately realize that you've made the right choice, for as your boots crunch into the skull and splinter it into a hundred pieces, the body ceases to move entirely. If it was air quotes "dead" before, it's capital D-E-A-D dead now, and the skeleton's hand has released its hold on the sword it was carrying. Not one to look a gift sword in the, er, mouth, you lean over and pick up the abandoned blade.

CONGRATULATIONS! YOU HAVE ACQUIRED

THE SWORD!

You slash the air around you with your newly acquired weapon, feeling its perfect balance and weight in your hand. It's comforting, like an old friend . . . which is funny, since it was previously owned by a reanimated corpse who definitely did NOT want to make friends. At any rate, you're happy to have it in your hand. And now that you have the sword, you feel that you can continue into the graveyard with at least a little bit of confidence and try to find your way out of this game.

Head to 76 ●●●

●●●

You swing your sword at the Abominable Snowmancer and CONNECT, striking the foul creature directly in its face. Unfortunately, your sword FREEZES upon contact and shatters, leaving you holding nothing but its grip, guard, and pommel. An icy smile spreads across the face of the Abominable Snowmancer as it reaches for you, grabbing you by the shoulders with both of its hands. Suddenly you feel colder than you've ever felt before, and it takes a moment before you realize that you are quickly being frozen solid. Too late you realize that the ice statues around you don't just LOOK like adventurers, they ARE adventurers. Or former ones. Well, now you know. And now . . .

YOU ARE DEAD. CONTINUE: Y/N?
Y: Head to 167 ● **N: Head to 242** ●●●

●●●●

You fall off the Skele-King and land in a heap on a pile of bones, which you will now join.

YOU ARE DEAD. CONTINUE: Y/N?
Y: Head to 167 ● N: Head to 242 ●●●

●

Hoping to anticipate the path of the Galactic Authority fighter, you close your eyes and attempt to feel its future path by instinct, which tells you to move to the right. But when you open your eyes, the fighter is gone. Closing your eyes? What were you thinking? Whatever it was, THINK AGAIN.

Head back to 69 ●

●●

Thinking to confuse the behemoth, you move to the left. But even though the monster looks slow, it moves surprisingly fast, bringing its improvised club down on you before you can think, *Perhaps I should have attacked . . .*

YOU ARE DEAD. CONTINUE: Y/N?
Y: Head to 196 ●● N: Head to 242 ●●●

●●●

C.O.B. shakes his cute little head—he's not going backward in any way, shape, or form. He moves ever forward to his goal, so try something else!

Head back to 119 ●●●●

●●●●

Moving in this direction was your first—and last—mistake, for you've piloted your Walker into a newly formed chasm in the floor of the jungle. As you plummet, your Walker collides with and scrapes against the sides of the hole you're falling down, and you try to grasp hold of anything that will arrest your momentum, but nothing works. There's no doubt about it . . .

YOU ARE DEAD. CONTINUE: Y/N?
Y: Head to 56 ●● **N:** Head to 242 ●●●

●

You're very good at swinging that sword at nothing, aren't you? If you're ever attacked by empty air, you are MORE than prepared to defend yourself.

Head back to 162 ●

●●

Even though you're nowhere near the center of the Slaystation, you decide that NOW would be a good time to unleash C.O.B.'s weapon. The little robot EXPLODES, taking the Spider-Bots with him, and then . . . nothing. The Slaystation itself is intact.

Sgt. Brixto looks at you and shakes his head.

"They're definitely going to bust you back down to cadet for this one. If any of us Space Pirates survive this battle, that is." And with the sound of Sgt. Brixto's disappointment ringing in your ears, you understand that it's the end.

Head to 242 ●●●

The Galactic Authority fighter has gone left, right, up, and down, but now it's directly in your sights.
What do you do?

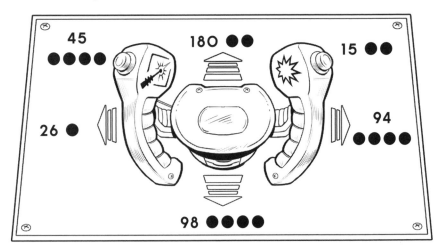

●●●●

You jump up onto the well cover, which, as it turns out, was a miscalculation—the wood is old and rotten, and your weight causes you to break through. You try to grab the lip of the well, but you fail and end up falling down . . . down . . . down . . . down . . .

Down . . . down . . . down . . . down . . . down . . .

SMACK!

You've hit the water far below and, thanks to your armor, you sink to the bottom.

YOU ARE DEAD. CONTINUE: Y/N?

Y: Head to 188 ● N: Head to 242 ●●●

●

C.O.B. crawls into the tunnel and, for a moment, makes progress. But the tunnel is obstructed by a tangle of wire and other trash, and C.O.B. becomes hopelessly entangled. As the Spider-Bots overtake and begin to savagely disassemble him, you realize that you've failed in your mission to destroy Slaystation Omega, and that it's the end.

Head to 242 ●●●

You try to head south, but the vines that lie across the path come to sinuous life, blocking you from going in that direction. Try a different way.

Head back to 136 ●●

●●●

Your Walker, armed with a massive club that used to be a tree trunk, is facing off against a Galactic Authority hover tank, which stands between you and any possibility of getting off this planet. Decision time is here. What do you do?

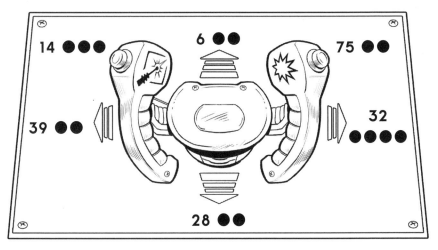

●●●●

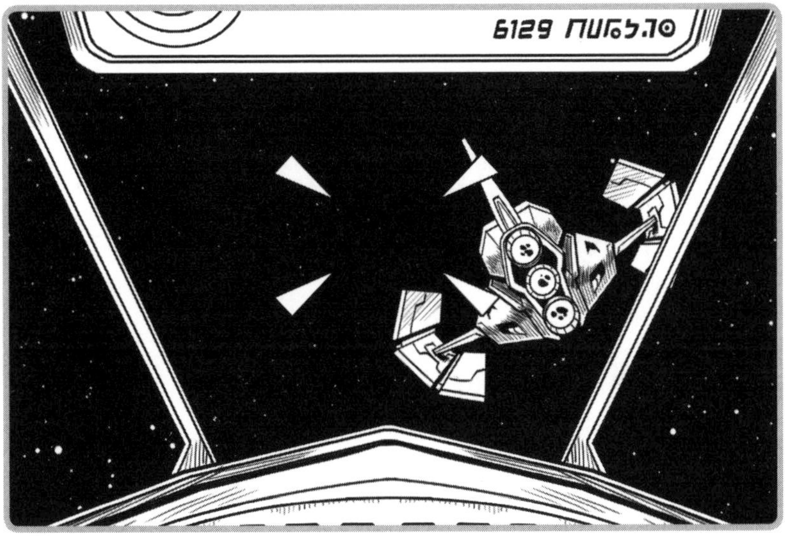

Somehow, you've managed to turn the tables on the Black Angel and almost have the villain in your crosshairs. ALMOST. The enemy ship is juking up and down, hoping to shake you. What's your next move, Cadet?

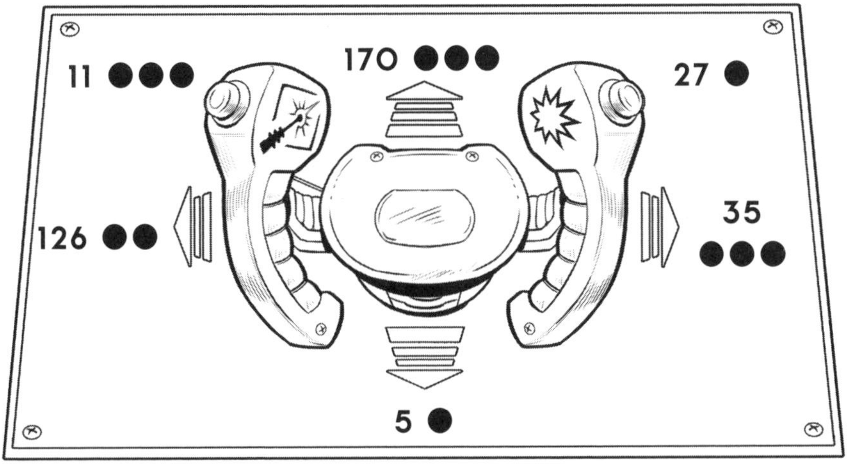
11 ●●●
170 ●●●
27 ●
126 ●●
35 ●●●
5 ●

●

You try to climb over the rubble and move down the center lane, but you can't make any headway. It's too steep, and you keep sliding back down to the ground of the plaza. You can't go this way. Not yet, at least.

Head back to 188 ●

●●

C.O.B. needs no help from you to keep running from the Spider-Bots. He's programmed to keep running and running and running. Select another move!

Head back to 119 ●●●●

●●●

This time, instead of running, you move slowwwwwly to the right. The Stone-King slowwwwwly turns its head to follow your progress.

"I could tell you what to do here," says the voice from the Almost-Bottomless Well. "Buuuut . . . I don't want to."

Vowing to shut that well up, you move back to where you were standing before—slowwwwwly—and make another move.

Head back to 110 ●●●

●●●●

The gate back to the graveyard is sealed. It probably won't open again until you finish a task here in the Abandoned Village. Best to try something else. Choose again.

Head back to 188 ●

●

Feeling reckless, you push C.O.B. to the left and head toward the fiery light. As it turns out, you've entered some sort of furnace room and are running down a dangerously narrow path that leads you over a pit of what looks to be molten metal. It looks very unsafe, but C.O.B. nimbly jogs along while the Spider-Bots follow.

Head to 119 ●●●●

●●

Fascinated by the idea of what sort of toys would have been sold in a weird town like this, you decide to poke around Ye Olde Toy Shoppe. As you pass the threshold, you hear the chime of a bell, as if it's alerting an unseen proprietor to your presence . . .

Head to 64 ●●

●●●

You move as deftly as you can to the right, but the skeleton anticipates your ruse and moves in front of you, blocking your way.

Head back to 184 ●

●●●●

You move C.O.B. to the left as the Galactic Authority troops begin to blast away at him. The swift robot deftly avoids their shots, but while he's dodging laser fire, the Spider-Bots overtake him, pinning him to the ground and brutally deactivating him. That's it. You've failed.

Head to 242 ●●●

●

You hit the Skele-King's legs with your sword, which only enrages it. Try again.

Head back to 114 ●●

●●

BRAAAP! Nothing happens. And while you were messing around, you lost sight of the fighter you were pursuing.

"Pay attention, Cadet!" screams Sgt. Brixto over the comms link. You begin scanning around, looking for the lost fighter . . .

Head back to 23 ●

●●●

You move to the left, and the dead eyes of every single toy in the shop follow your motion. Creepy, but they don't do anything else. Choose again.

Head back to 64 ●●

●●●●

You pull the Gorillosaur back, hoping to flip it over in a feat of Walker mech martial arts, but your attempt at fancy footwork falls flat as you fall on your back with the Gorillosaur over you. You try to get up, but the creature has other plans as it reaches for the cockpit . . . and YOU. Using its powerful claws, it cracks open your cockpit like it's a pistachio shell, and then it reaches for the delicious nut inside.

You. You're the nut. And . . .

YOU ARE DEAD. CONTINUE: Y/N?
Y: Head to **68** ●●●● **N:** Head to **242** ●●●

●

You run to the right, but pieces of the Skele-King's marble slab tombstone block your way. You'll have to figure out something else!

Head back to 114 ●●

●●

Foolishly, you decide to attack the hulking Stone-King, and it laughs as you fruitlessly try to chop at its wood-and-rock body. But still . . . you're alive!

Head to 99 ●

●●●

You press the button to shoot your lasers, but all C.O.B. does is shrug—he can't do that! All he can do is run, evade, and explode, so stick to that and choose again.

Head back to 119 ●●●●

● ● ● ●

Your sword cuts the air, smiting an invisible enemy.
Practice is a good habit. Keep it up (but choose a
direction to travel in).

Head back to 76 ● ● ●

●

Turning around and moving back toward the gate does
nothing—it's locked tight and you can't go that way.
Forget that plan and come up with something new.

Head back to 167 ●

● ●

You try to back up, hoping to stall for time, but you trip
over a stray skull and fall on your back. Before you can
recover, the Skele-King advances and grabs you, pinning
your arms to your sides. You only have a moment to
reflect on what you would have done differently before
the Skele-King's blade whizzes through the air toward
your neck and . . .

YOU ARE DEAD. CONTINUE: Y/N?
Y: Head to 167 ●   N: Head to 242 ● ● ●

●●●

Everything around you starts to quickly disassemble into digital noise, until for a brief moment everything goes white, and you're . . .

. . . inside the mall, but just outside the entrance of the Midnight Arcade, which is now closed and completely dark inside. Looking through the dusty windows of the arcade, you can see only the shadows of the game cabinets covered by plastic tarps. You bang on the glass, hoping to get the attention of the guy who greeted you, but there's no one there. Like the rest of the mall, the place is entirely devoid of life.

Shoulders slumping, you head back to where you entered the Fair Oaks Mall, slipping through its front door and trotting across the empty parking lot where your friends wait with expectant looks on their faces. You hop the fence and drop to the ground, and they surround you, peppering you with questions.

"What was it like?"

"Did you see any ghosts?"

"Was it scary?"

"Did you even go past the food court? You were only gone for five minutes."

Five minutes? That can't be right. You were inside

those games for HOURS, it seems, but here you are.

You shake your head, certain that you weren't dreaming, but what proof do you have?

"Aw, jeez," somebody says, looking at their phone. "My mom's gonna kill me if she catches me out this late. We'd better bail."

Everybody hops on their bikes and begins to ride away, but you pause, still unsure about what happened, and glance back at the mall. Still empty-looking. Still vacant. Despite everything you remember, you figure you must have had some sort of weird waking dream. You reach into your pocket to check your phone but feel something unfamiliar in there, something small, round, and metallic. Once you take it out, your eyes grow wide.

It's a token from the MIDNIGHT ARCADE.

You clutch the strange souvenir tightly in your fist and jam it back into your pocket. Ha! It WAS real after all. Everything DID happen. As you lean into your bike pedals, picking up speed and catching up to your friends, you promise yourself that some night soon you'll come back here. Why? Because it's one of the rules of video gaming: A good game deserves a sequel. You smile to yourself, knowing that this is not . . .

THE END.